March 1994

⟨ T5-DGV-109

WITHDRAWN

LARGE PRINT
MAINE STATE LIBRARY
STATION 64
AUGUSTA ME 04333

WINTHROP, MAINE

The Mayeroni Myth

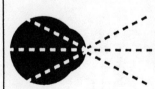

This Large Print Book carries the
Seal of Approval of N.A.V.H.

The Mayeroni Myth

Daoma Winston

Thorndike Press • Thorndike, Maine

Library of Congress Cataloging in Publication Data:

Winston, Daoma, 1922-
    The Mayeroni myth / Daoma Winston.
        p. cm.
    ISBN 1-56054-279-9 (alk. paper : lg. print)
    1. Large type books. I. Title.
[PS3545.I7612M39   1992]   91-34947
813'.54—dc20   CIP

Copyright © 1972 by Daoma Winston.
All rights reserved.

Thorndike Press Large Print edition published in 1992
by arrangement with Jay Garon-Brooke Associates, Inc.

Cover photo by Alan LaVallee.

The tree indicium is a trademark of Thorndike Press.

This book is printed on acid-free, high opacity paper.

The Mayeroni Myth

Chapter 1

Fabriana and I were linked together by bonds stronger than any fabric grown or made, by the bonds of blood and bone and gene.

We were always the same, so that when I looked at her I saw myself.

Yet we were always different, too.

Even now, after all the time that has passed, I wonder how it came about, and why. I wonder what she really intended . . .

I was working when I heard the postman shuffle through the maple leaves on the path, and then mount the two front steps to the cottage.

I didn't really want to stop. The morning light was perfect, and the brush felt like an extension of my fingers. My eyes seemed finally to perceive those colors I had first seen in my mind. It was a good time for going on and on, for exploiting the surge of creativity while it lasted, for watching the canvas come alive.

Instead, with a quick sigh, I thrust the brush into the turpentine jar, rubbed my paint-stained hands on my hips, where the habitual gesture had already left stiff colorful patches, and went quickly to the front door.

Mr. Pierce was as accustomed to our brief morning chats as I was. They were a ritual begun just a little over two years before, while I was twelve feet off the ground and teetering on a recalcitrant ladder. He had come along the path through spring sun, and tipped his wizened face to peer at me through quizzical blue eyes.

"Don't move. Don't breathe," he ordered, and disappeared down the lane.

It was easier to say than to do. I braced myself to fall through empty air. But within what seemed the same instant he was back. He bracketed the ladder with heavy stones, then dusted his hands and rose smiling.

I climbed down to thank him, but he waved my gratitude aside, saying dryly, "A little girl like you oughtn't to be scampering about on ladders. I've been wondering who took the place over. Now I know. Welcome. Very welcome indeed. Those shutters have needed a painting for the last ten years."

Thus, quickly and surely, he had become my first friend in the small New England town to which I had come as a stranger.

That was why, I suppose, I couldn't ignore his friendly whistle, even though, at the moment, I would have preferred to continue the momentum of my work.

Now, when I opened the door to him, he grinned widely enough to rearrange the deep wrinkles on his brow. "You get a real haul today, Cecily. Lots of ads, of course. Send them right into the circular file. You don't care about that junk. But there's also something from the place in New York. Your business place, I mean. Maybe it means good news." He stopped expectantly.

By my business place he meant the gallery that showed, and sold, a few of my paintings. He knew with how much anxiety I always opened letters from Ryson and Davis.

"Oh, let's see what they say," I said, eagerly opening the envelope he gave me. I was elated to find a check for a hundred dollars, along with a very encouraging note from Henry Ryson. The day, already so well begun, was suddenly even brighter. "You're good luck to me, Mr. Pierce," I laughed.

His eyes twinkled. "Maybe I can do better than that." He made a gesture, a magician pulling a rabbit out of a tall silk hat. "There's this, too." He thrust a small blue envelope at me, and went on, "I didn't know you had any family, Cecily. Much less in Florida. Somehow I always thought you were alone in the world. Like me." Again he waited expectantly.

9

I *was* alone in the world. I wanted to be.

It had taken pain, and a stubbornness I hadn't known I possessed, to gain my freedom. But now a quick pulse began to beat in my throat.

I said, "I don't have any relatives. At least not in Florida. No, not there," and looked down at the small blue envelope, but didn't open it.

"It's going to be a fine fall day," Mr. Pierce told me after a moment.

I nodded silent agreement, but my eyes were fixed on the envelope that seemed to burn my grimy fingers. The curlicues and loops and doughnuts for dots were familiar. I knew the hand that had formed them as well as I knew my own. I didn't need to look at the return address to know who had written it.

"Well," Mr. Pierce drawled, "I guess I better finish the rounds, Cecily. Now don't start painting your shutters again while I'm away."

It was a hoary joke by now, but I always found it pleasant to laugh with him over the memory of our first meeting.

This morning, though, prickles of uneasiness scampered along my arms, and the sunshine suddenly paled.

"I won't do any shutters," I promised, forcing myself to smile, though my lips felt tight

10

and cold. Although I didn't know why then, perhaps I was answering a premonition when I added, "See you tomorrow, Mr. Pierce."

He repeated with certainty, "See you tomorrow sure," and kicked through the carpet of golden leaves, and disappeared down the lane.

The moment he was gone, I wished that I had kept him with me for another few moments at least. Somehow I didn't want to be alone. Alone to face the problems of the past, problems I had thought outgrown and resolved forever.

When I went inside the door slapped shut behind me with a click of finality. I leaned against it, eyeing the blue envelope again. If only I could blow it away with a casual breath. With proper magic, I told myself, I could make the envelope gone, make even the memory of it gone.

In the absence of proper magic, I could throw it away. I sighed, went into the kitchen. I put the stack of mail on the table, then took the small blue square and slid it carefully into the trash bin under the sink.

At that moment the sun edged around the window frame, filling the kitchen with a warm brassy glow. I told myself to get back to work now that the light was good again. Instead, I rewarmed the leftover breakfast coffee. When

11

I poured it into the cup, I noticed that my hand was trembling.

I drank the coffee too quickly, scalding my lips and tongue. The small pain stayed with me as my eyes made a continual track across the room to the trash bin, and the quick pulse continued to beat in my throat.

Impatient with myself, I rose. I went to the small mirror over the sink, and regarded the image that looked back at me.

Deep-set hazel eyes, slanted slightly beneath sharp winging dark brows, seemed to fill the face. The cheeks were very lightly tanned, defined by faint hollows. The chin was small and square. The hair was very long, and dark enough to hold hints of raven gloss. That was the face I knew.

I was small, quite slender. I had been told that I looked fragile. But in fact I was robust and active and had always been.

I was twenty-two years old, but often, in blue jeans and shirt, I looked somewhat younger.

But now, aware of the blue envelope I had thrown away, I looked much older.

I felt older, too.

It was a familiar sensation, come back to me from the past I had tried to forget. My shoulders sagged beneath an unseen burden. My muscles grew taut, as if straining in effort.

The air became thin, so that every breath was a struggle.

I had thought it was finished.

It had been two years, so I had allowed myself to begin to hope.

I had always believed that everyone in the world needed, and was entitled to a certain freedom. I thought everyone had to stand on his own feet, to find himself and be himself.

I had tried to make what I believed into a living reality.

But now there was the glimmer of a specter in the cottage I had so lovingly furnished. I felt its presence spread and grow, rooting itself in the place that was mine. It reached for me from the blue envelope with the looped and curlicued address written in Fabriana's hand.

Fabriana . . .

The name was a whisper in my mind. The image that filled it was my own image, the physical embodiment of my other self. Fabriana was my sister, my twin, younger by ten minutes, but identical in every overt measure.

Fabriana . . . the specter from the past.

I shivered and turned from the mirror. I went into the studio, resolutely bent on going back to work. Painting was my life now, and the small verbal and financial encouragement that I received from Ryson and Davis meant everything to me. But my earlier elation was gone as if it had never warmed me. And the room was lemon pale, with a damp autumn mist hanging at the rim of the windows.

I stood before the easel. The colors in which I had gloried before seemed suddenly flat and stale. I couldn't remember what I had imagined before. I couldn't recall the sureness and excitement I had felt then. I sighed and turned away.

It was the letter from Fabriana, of course.

Through it she reached out to me.

I found myself remembering the last time I had seen her. It was two years earlier. Our parents had been killed in an automobile accident several months before. They had been traveling together, as always, she a concert pianist on tour, he her manager, and artist by avocation.

Fabriana and I had been brought up to the sound of thunderous background music pouring from our mother's practice room, and the gentle whispers of the long line of governesses who took care of us. The two of us were constants in an ever-changing environment.

Fabriana was shaken by those early insecurities, and clung to me ever tighter.

I was strengthened, and determined to free myself.

Once the first shock of being orphaned had

14

dulled, I decided that Fabriana and I must separate.

It might seem cruel, but it was a decision arrived at through pain, and as much in love as in the need for survival.

It was only when I had made my decision that I told Fabriana what I intended to do. She refused to believe me until the day I packed my bags.

Then she stood watching, white-faced, trembling. "You can't do it, Cecily," she said finally. "We've always been together. It was meant to be. You can't go away and leave me alone. You can't abandon me."

I hardened myself against the sudden ache of pity. I had expected it. I had been prepared.

Fabriana's voice grew shrill. "Mother and Father will curse you for it. You'll be sorry. Wait and see. You'll be sorry you ran away from me."

I said, as gently as I could, "Fabriana, we're both grown up now. We're twenty years old. We can't cling together like frightened children. We've nothing to be frightened of, and we're not children."

Fabriana's deep-set hazel eyes glittered with those easy tears that I knew she had learned long ago to control. She peered at me from beneath disarrayed dark bangs.

When, a month earlier, I had impulsively had my long hair cut and re-styled, Fabriana had wept, too, and then immediately had her own hair cut and shaped to match my own. She had never been able to allow me any slight difference. If I attempted it, she immediately copied me. It had always been that way.

But it wasn't the small act alone of course that had convinced me. That small act had been the symbol to which I clung as I made my plans.

Ever since I could remember, Fabriana had insisted on stressing our so-obvious twin-hood. We were physically identical, and she was determined that, in even those superficial ways in which I could maintain my own individuality, we would remain identical. Outwardly alike as two peas in a pod, there was this difference between us. I needed to stand on my own. Fabriana needed to cling. I was independent, self-reliant, outgoing. Fabriana was just the opposite in every way.

She was abetted by our parents, perhaps unconsciously. They were amused by the admiring exclamations of people who saw us together. They assumed that because we had each other we could never be lonely, which lightened the weight of responsibility on them.

"But I won't know what to do," Fabriana

had faltered, that day while I was packing. "How shall I live? Where can I go?"

She wore a white sleeveless shirt, and a blue skirt. She had a silver bracelet on her wrist. She had watched me dress that morning, and followed suit. I had already known what I was going to do.

I told her then, "You must decide what you want to do, Fabriana. I think I'll find some place where it won't cost too much to live and settle down to try to paint."

"But what about me?"

I smiled faintly, "You'll manage all right."

Plainly she didn't want my reassurance. She cried, "I can't. I won't. I don't even know where to begin." Her tears made silvery trails down her lightly tanned cheeks.

I didn't answer her.

"If Mother and Father hadn't died you wouldn't be doing this," she screamed at me.

"I don't mean to hurt you," I told her. "And I don't know what I'd do if things were different, Fabriana. But this is how things are."

I didn't really know what I would have done if our parents had lived. They had never understood my need to separate myself from Fabriana. They had, I conceded to myself, never really known Fabriana. They had never been quite sure which of us was which. That had amused Fabriana and hurt me. Fabriana had frequently made use of their confusion. I had always resented it.

Delighted with twins, with the stir they made when they paraded their two pretty girls, they had always dressed us alike. They never understood why I, at fourteen, refused to shop any longer with Fabriana. They thought it funny when Fabriana doggedly waited until I had chosen my own clothes and then carefully outfitted herself in exactly the same things from shoes to hair ribbons. They never understood when I, having painted since I was a tiny child, stopped painting because Fabriana insisted on copying whatever I did, sometimes even stealing my work and passing it off as her own. They never understood why I began to refuse dates with neighborhood boys because Fabriana pursued the same ones, sometimes pretending that she was me. They never understood that I felt as if one part of me belonged to Fabriana.

We were identical, but not the same. It had always been completely obvious to me, though to no one else. I needed to be free. Fabriana needed to be a twin. I thought of myself as a whole person. Fabriana thought of herself as only a part person.

And yet, I, the older by just ten minutes, had always been forced to accept the role of

18

protector. Chafing, impatient, but too loving to refuse Fabriana the support and care she required, I had been mother and father and older sister to Fabriana for as long as I could remember. I was made very aware of this at our parents' death. I saw that Fabriana was untouched and unshaken. I blamed myself. I had allowed Fabriana to lean on me. Now Fabriana must learn to stand alone. But that was only a part of it. I couldn't, even to myself, pretend otherwise. I knew that *I* wanted to stand alone.

I fought back doubt, and pity, and finished packing. I took my things to the door, turned back to say, "Goodbye, Fabriana, I'll write as soon as I'm settled."

"But what should I do?" she wailed.

I said patiently, "We both of us have the small incomes we were left. They'll make nice secure nest eggs. But they won't stretch very far. I think you should get a job, think of some way of earning more, and meanwhile spend your time usefully and interestingly."

Fabriana stared at me for a moment. Her hazel eyes were suddenly dry, the silver trails gone from her cheeks. "All right," she said. "Go on, Cecily, go on and leave me. But don't bother to write. I don't want to know where you are. I don't want ever to see you again. I'll never talk to you, or care about you. Or need you. Not as long as I live."

The strained coldness in her voice communicated itself to me in a chill of goose flesh on my arms. I hesitated for a moment, then I said firmly, "I'll write to you."

I stayed in New York for a short time. That was when I made my contact with Henry Ryson. I wrote to Fabriana from there. I wrote her again when I settled in my small cottage, with my easel and paints, and my very few friends. But Fabriana had never replied.

In the two years gone by, I had begun to believe that perhaps Fabriana had found herself. Perhaps now, alone and on her own, she had begun to understand what it was that had driven me away. Perhaps she had been right, even the stronger, in insisting on the clean though painful break. I had thought that some day we could be sisters again when we were both sure enough of ourselves.

But now, looking at the canvas before me and not seeing it, I shivered.

Yes, I had hoped. Still, the moment I saw Fabriana's handwriting, I had been frightened. I had thrown the letter away. I had been afraid to read it lest the relationship finally broken be reestablished by a few words.

With a shamed sigh I turned away from the easel.

I went into the kitchen, took the letter

from the trash bin.

Surely it wouldn't hurt to know what Fabriana said, to learn where she was living, and how, to know if the frozen coldness had been melted by time.

As I slid a careful nail under the flap to open the envelope, I realized that I could never have thrown it away. I could only try, perhaps pretend to try. I would never have succeeded. I had waited too long to hear from Fabriana, thought of her too often, to turn away from the small overture she had made at last.

Her letter was dated two days before. She wrote:

Cecily dear, I didn't mean all those things I said when you went away. I'm sorry. I didn't understand. But I do now. I need you, Cecily. I'm in terrible trouble. You have to help me. You have to. Please, please, no matter what, drop everything and come here. It's a matter of life or death. Mine, Cecily. You don't hate me, do you? Come to me here, Cecily, and wear a blonde wig. Nobody will even know that we're related, much less twins. Please come. Hurry. The Seaside Motel in Key West. I'll be registered. Just ask for me. Wire me at the motel when you'll arrive. And hurry.

The shaky signature was a big black sprawl across the bottom of the blue sheet. *Fabriana*

The words seemed to blur and flicker on the sheet. I read them again, then once more. A matter of life and death. Mine. Wear a blonde wig. Nobody will know we're even related, much less twins. Wire me when you'll be arriving.

I had hoped for reassurance, for the possibility of a new relationship between us. But this, this was the old Fabriana, crying out to me.

My hands tightened around the letter. I crumpled it into a ball, flung it away from me.

No, I told myself. No. No. And heard myself whisper aloud, "Oh, Fabriana, I'm sorry. I can't. I can't do it."

I pulled on a sweater and went out into the yard. The lemon pale sun had disappeared behind low hanging mists. I raked great heaps of golden leaves and watched the light wind disperse them. Autumn came early in the village. There would soon be many chores to do in preparation for the long cold winter ahead. I went inside and dusted the cottage from top to bottom. I neatened the closets, then straightened the dresser drawers. I rearranged the cupboard as I'd been planning to do for several months.

With me, as I went about the homely tasks

that I usually enjoyed, went the memory of Fabriana's words, the plea for help that sounded so . . . so exaggerated, yet so honestly frightened.

At last, unwillingly, I took up the crumpled letter. I smoothed it out, reread its words again.

I knew that I must not go. In fairness to us both I must ignore Fabriana's call.

But even then I was busy making plans.

I called the small airport which served the five villages in the area, and arranged a flight to Boston, a change for a Miami plane, another change for Key West. Fortunately it wasn't the tourist season, so seats were easily arranged.

I wired Fabriana at the Seaside Motel.

Mr. Pierce drove me to the airport. I left the cottage key with him so that he could water my plants. Everything else was prepared for an absence. I had unconsciously attended to that even before I made up my mind to go. I took with me only a small weekend case, containing pajamas, and a single change of dress. I was determined to be back in no more than a day or two.

At nine o'clock that same evening, I stepped off the plane into the balmy autumn warmth of Key West.

The brilliant stars hung close, small chips of twinkling light that formed patterns man had studied since time began.

The cab took me down a wide boulevard lined with high white stucco walls, from which the shadows of exotic trees seemed to beckon.

They registered on my consciousness, and I still remember my first sight of them, but at the same time I was trying to control the alarm I felt. Soon I would see Fabriana. Soon I would know.

The motel room clerk was a plump, dark middle-aged man. When I asked for Fabriana, he frowned at me long and thoughtfully.

I wondered if the wig I had managed to find in Boston had slipped sideways, and patted it carefully. I wondered if he saw through it to the hair beneath it and was abashed by a resemblance he didn't understand.

I gave him what I hoped was an imperious stare, asked, "Miss Harden is in, isn't she?"

His frown disappeared. His dark eyes narrowed in a smile. "You bet. She's been in all day. It's Cottage 10, through that door. Think you can find it? Or you want me to walk you back?"

"I'll find it," I told him.

I walked through a yard of palms lit by pink and yellow and red lights, and blossom-thick poincianas, past a family of plastic herons, and around a small brightly glowing tropical fish.

I found Cottage 10.

I took a deep breath, said a small silent prayer, and then I knocked gently.

Fabriana flung open the door, cried, "Oh, Cecily, Cecily, why did it take you so terribly long?" and burst into tears.

Chapter 2

I stepped inside, closed the door behind me.

I saw no reason to expose the both of us to any watching eyes that might be about. I remembered too vividly what Fabriana had written to take any unnecessary risks until I understood what was troubling her.

She looked exactly the same as when I had last seen her. Her dark bangs were disarrayed, and her cheeks were wet with tears. But now she wore a white blouse and a very short white skirt, both rather wrinkled, as if she had been lying down in them.

"It hasn't been long," I told her gently. "I just received your letter this morning, you know."

"But it seemed like . . . like years," Fabriana wept. "I was so afraid, so terribly afraid that you wouldn't come. And if you hadn't . . . oh, Cecily, you don't know. You just don't realize . . ."

But it was some time before she could collect herself. She huddled in the big gray easy chair before the television set, and cried, and muttered incoherent words, from which I could make no sense at all.

I finally gave up trying.

I knew that she would calm down and explain in her own good time.

Meanwhile I decided to make myself more comfortable.

I took off the thick heavy blonde wig and set it aside. It was a relief to comb out my long hair. In the mirror, past my shoulder, I saw Fabriana watching me. I turned then.

"Yes," I said. "I let it grow out again. I decided I didn't like it short after all."

"As soon as you got away from me," Fabriana whispered.

"Not quite that soon." I managed a smile. "Now then, suppose you tell me . . . "

"It doesn't matter. We can cut your hair. Thank goodness it wasn't the other way around. That might have presented a problem."

She didn't give me a chance to ask her what she was talking about. She went on, "I guess you're anxious to know why I wrote you?"

"I'm anxious to know what you're afraid of, and why you felt you needed me," I admitted.

"Just like that," she whispered. "That's all you can think of." She straightened up, her eyes bright and clear and thoughtful, all tears gone now. "We haven't seen each other for two years, and you come in here as if you were a stranger, not a sister, not a twin, but a stranger, and start demanding to know . . . "

I gave her a faint smile, hoping to cover an uneasiness I couldn't repress. "You wrote that it was a matter of life or death to you, remember? Naturally I'd be anxious . . . "

"Oh, we'll talk about that later," Fabriana answered. "Right now I want to know about you. What you've been doing, and who you know, and . . . oh, everything, everything, Cecily."

Her eyes had become even brighter, almost feverish in their intensity. Her smile came and went. I knew her in that mood. The best way to handle it had always been to go along with her. Besides, I admitted to myself, I was just as curious about her as she was about me.

I said, "You wouldn't believe how hungry I am, Fabriana. Let's talk about it all over dinner."

"You're still so practical," she complained, smiling still.

"There must be a decent restaurant around here somewhere. Couldn't we . . . "

"Oh, no, no, what are you thinking of? We can't go out. Not together. Nobody should see us together." Fabriana jumped up. "I'll go. I'll bring some sandwiches in, and some soda, or coffee, whatever you want." She gave an eager laugh. "We'll have a picnic in the cottage. Just like old times, Cecily."

"But what is this business about nobody seeing us together? And then, the blonde wig . . . I felt so ridiculous. And it's the most uncomfortable thing I've ever had on my head in my life. That anyone who saw me would think I . . . "

"Would think you were me," Fabriana finished. "Surely that's obvious. Or will be. And that's what I want. But if there were the two of us, together, then . . . " She was at the door, nervously tapping her foot by then. She flashed me a quick smile. "You said you were hungry. I'll be right back."

She was gone before I could protest.

But I had learned one thing. The blonde wig was to keep a casual observer from realizing that I was Fabriana's twin sister.

While I uneasily considered that, I took my things from my weekend case and freshened up. By the time I had finished, Fabriana returned.

She gave me another bright eager smile as she put hamburgers and fried onion rings on the round table next to the gray chair. "You see? I knew exactly what you'd want. I didn't have to ask."

I smiled back at her, unable to resist her warmth. "You ought to. We've both eaten

29

hamburgers and onion rings all our lives."

"And . . ." With a flourish, she produced cherry soda. "I'll bet you haven't had this for a long time."

I hadn't. I didn't tell Fabriana that I had lost my taste for cherry soda along the way.

But she said, tilting her dark head so that raven wings slid along her cheek, "You might have changed, Cecily. I think maybe you have changed."

"I might have. Why not? In two years one does."

She shuddered. "All right. Don't remind me. Oh, Cecily, it was so awful of you to go away like that. Do you know, for days and days, I couldn't stop crying? I just didn't know what to do."

"You finally did figure it out," I retorted. "You must have. Because you've survived. And you're here."

"Yes, I'm here." Fabriana frowned. "And that's just it."

"Then tell me." I bit into my hamburger with relish, but my attention was fixed on her.

"It's hard to know where to begin."

"At the beginning?"

"The thing is . . . I don't know how . . . I just can't be sure . . ."

I waited.

She examined her hamburger as if she

30

might find the answer to her confusion there. At last she looked up at me. "No, Cecily. You go first. Tell me everything that's happened to you."

I didn't intend to do that. It didn't seem necessary. But I told her about Ryson and Davis, and the few pictures they had sold for me. I described the cottage, the village in which I lived. I told her about Mr. Pierce, my other friends there.

"You did just what you wanted to do," she said, having listened thoughtfully.

"What I had to do, Fabriana."

"Sure. Sure, I know that."

"And what about you?"

She shrugged. "I did the same. Just what I had to do. When I finally stopped crying, I pulled myself together. I looked around for something. It's a good thing you had taken typing, Cecily. Because that's why I took it. Anyway, it came in handy. I got one typing job, and then another. The second brought me to Miami, on a business trip. Then the job I have now turned up, and that brought me here." She stopped, took a deep breath. Then she went on, "The thing is, Cecily, I don't want you to get mad at me and go running off again. You see? That's the trouble. That's what I'm afraid of. That's why I find it so hard all of a sudden to get started."

31

"I came because you needed me," I said slowly. "Isn't that enough?"

Fabriana's bright gaze slid away from mine. "Oh, of course it is." She paused, shivered violently. "Okay. Here goes. I work for a man named Dwayne Fuller, and live with him and his family on Skeleton Key. Which is just off Key West. I'm his secretary, his typist. All that."

I nodded.

Her small frail hands twisted nervously. "The thing is I don't have much time now. Not to give you all the crazy details, I mean. Because . . . because I'm supposed to be back there first thing tomorrow morning. Somebody will meet me at the marina with a launch. It's the only way to get to Skeleton Key. I came in to town for a few days shopping, and to see a girl friend, I told them all, and I wrote to you, and oh, Cecily, I daren't go back. I can't. I just can't!"

I waited expectantly, but she didn't say any more. Finally I asked, "But why?"

"It's so complicated. I don't know how to explain . . . I . . . "

"You don't have to go back if you don't want to," I told her. "You have experience now. I'm sure you can find another job. Just let Dwayne Fuller know, and . . . "

"Oh, he's a wonderful man," Fabriana

cried. "But it isn't the job. It's . . . " She stopped, drew a deep hard breath. "Listen, Cecily, the reason I wrote to you . . . what I want . . . Well, I want you to take my place on Skeleton Key. I want you to figure out what's going on, and set it right."

"Fabriana!" I gasped. "What a strange suggestion!"

She ignored my protest, hurried on, "Don't say no. Not yet. That's just what I was afraid of. Just listen to me. If you don't, I'll die, Cecily. I'll surely be killed, no matter where I go, or what I do." She stopped then, her chest heaving with quick breaths. The sound of them was loud in the sudden silence.

I put aside my unfinished sandwich. I wasn't hungry any more. I didn't want anything but an explanation. I told her that.

"I can't explain it very well. I don't know how. I don't really understand what's happening. But you'll be able to. If you were there, living with them, you'd be able to handle it. You'd manage the way you always do. You'd be inside, you see. But you'd have the perspective of the outsider."

"I see that you've thought it through," I told her. "But you still haven't told me what I'm to manage."

"Do you have to keep asking questions?" she cried. "Can't you just trust me, understand me? Can't you just help me, Cecily?"

I sighed. I felt as if we were both back where we had started from. Yet I couldn't turn my back on her now. Not when she had said it was a matter of life or death. I said, "Fabriana, I have to know what's wrong, don't I?"

She flung herself back in the chair. She gave me a panic-stricken look, whispered, "There's so little time. Really, Cecily, so little time left. And there's so much I have to tell you, and so much I have to do."

I folded my hands in my lap, and waited silently. I had come too far in answer to her plea to leave her without finding out why she had written to me. I knew that if I were patient I would eventually be able to make sense out of what Fabriana told me.

She said uneasily, "Anyhow, that's what I want. For you to stay on Skeleton Key. Just for a couple of weeks. You can spare a couple of weeks, can't you? To save my life?"

"If I knew how it was threatened," I told her. But I heard an echo in my voice that I recognized from other places and other times. I sensed in myself that familiar tightening against Fabriana's demands, the resistance against her hunger.

She must have heard it, too. Her eyes flickered at me. Then she said, "You'll do it,

34

Cecily. I know you will. I told you about Dwayne Fuller, the man I've worked for all during the past year. He's around fifty-five or so. Attractive. A widower." A smile glimmered faintly on her lips, then disappeared. "He's an archaeologist. He, and the rest of them, went on an expedition to Yucatan. They came back to Skeleton Key about a year and a half ago, I guess, and he's been writing a book about it ever since." For a moment, she paused. Then, "And that's why he needs me. And why I like the job so much, too. It's interesting. Well, there's him, you see." She went on, giving a careful physical description of him. "Then there's Mark Winstead. Now he . . ."

For the next two hours, Fabriana spoke. Her words came calmly now, slowly, softly.

It was, I thought, as if a hypnotic current flowed between the two of us, making it possible for me to see with my own eyes what Fabriana described. Skeleton Key, the tiny off-shore coral island on which Dwayne Fuller lived; his daughter, twenty-four-year-old Karen; his sister, fortyish unmarried Charlotte; his photographer, Hank Darrow; the ghost writer working with him, Mark Winstead; plump Rosa, the housekeeper and servant of all trades.

I began to feel as if I myself had already

35

been there, observing and learning and becoming part of the place. The very thought frightened me.

At last Fabriana's voice faded away. She gave me a level look.

"It sounds interesting, Fabriana. But . . ."

"But what?" she asked, her voice hoarse from so much talking without rest.

"You haven't given me a clue to what's really important. To why you said you were in danger, to why you wrote that it was a matter of life or death. I almost feel as if I know all these people, but I don't have the vaguest idea of what it adds up to."

"I can't explain that," Fabriana retorted.

"But why not? Why not?"

"I just can't," she told me sullenly.

I thought it over. She wanted me to take her place on Skeleton Key. She had said her life was in danger. If I took her place then my life would be in danger. I wondered if she realized what she was asking. I wondered why she wouldn't tell me what she *really* feared.

I said quietly, "You want me to masquerade as you. You say you're in danger. Then, as you, I'll be in danger, won't I?"

Her eyes flickered at me again and then quickly hid beneath drooping lids. She said firmly, "Only you can save me. If you will. If you want to." When I didn't answer her, she

36

went on, "You'll be all right. You can take care of yourself."

"We both know there's more to this than you're telling me," I insisted. "I won't make any promise to you, not until I know it all, Fabriana."

I heard the unyielding note in my voice. She heard it, too.

She let a few moments pass. Then she said, sulkily and coldly, "Oh, okay, Cecily, I guess I might as well tell you the whole truth, and nothing but the truth, so help me God. It's not that I'm really in trouble, nor in any danger, nor anything quite as dramatic as that. I thought, mistakenly, that you'd do anything to help me. So I said that."

I controlled a quick rush of anger, only half believing her now. "You pretended to be frightened? You pretended to need me? You brought me down here, worried about you, and scared, for nothing at all?"

"Oh, no, no, Cecily. I do need help. Terribly, terribly. I just have to get away from Skeleton Key for a couple of weeks. That's what it is. I just have to. But I don't want to lose my job with Dwayne. So I thought, if you . . . " She gave me an embarrassed smile. "And now you're going to ask me why I want to get away. Okay, I'll tell you. You see, there's this man . . . and I love him so much.

37

But it can't last. It won't. Just two weeks, Cecily, two weeks out of your life. And then . . . "

I knew that she wasn't telling me the truth. I allowed my disbelief to show in my face.

"Why don't you trust me?" she cried.

The cold words hung between us.

I shivered. I couldn't answer her. To answer meant to go digging into the past, raking up incidents long buried, hopefully forgiven and forgotten.

"It isn't so much, is it?" she asked suddenly. "You're happy in what you're doing, and settled, and successful. So why can't you give me two tiny weeks that would make it possible for me to be the same way. Please, please. Just that, and I'll never ask anything of you again. We'll both be quits again. Forever and ever if you want it that way."

"But I don't," I protested. "I wrote you several times. You never answered."

"You left me," she retorted. "You're the one that left. Not me." Then, voice softening, "But never mind that, Cecily. What's important is right now. I told you that they expect me back in the morning. We have an awful lot to do and talk about. So decide. Decide right now, and . . . "

"And you're going to go away with some man," I said.

38

She nodded. "Yes, yes, oh, it means so much to me. Please . . ."

I didn't really believe her. I was certain that she had left something out. Something important. The real reason that she wanted two weeks away from Skeleton Key.

"If you don't want to help me . . ."

I shook my head, trying to think through the little that she *had* told me.

She said, "We can cut your hair short again, style it like mine. Oh, it's a good thing you haven't gotten yourself too tan or too pale. Because we couldn't do much about that, could we? Oh, yes, we'll have to remember that I always wear more makeup than you do these days. And false eyelashes. And of course we'll just switch clothes. That won't be any problem."

"Wait. I haven't agreed . . ."

She grinned. "You will. I know you won't let me down, Cecily."

"But when would we switch back? How? Where?"

"Here, of course. And in two weeks, just as I said." Her grin widened. "Really. It'll be fun for you. A new experience." Her hazel eyes shone. She jumped to her feet, laughing. "Oh, I knew it, Cecily. I always could depend on you, and I knew I could depend on you this time, too."

39

I don't know exactly when or how I agreed to do as Fabriana asked. It seemed to me that one moment I was still trying to understand, to see through the lies, to delve into her hidden motives. And the next moments were filled with the sound of scissors snipping at my hair.

It was all somehow accomplished.

Meanwhile Fabriana talked. She said, "You know, Cecily, you'd better practice some more with the false lashes. And, oh, yes, stop and visit with Enrico for a few minutes in the morning. I always do. He'll expect it." She paused, then went on dreamily, "And in two weeks, I'll phone a reservation in for Cottage 10. And you meet me. And then everything will be all right. Oh, yes, it will. I'm not expecting to work for Dwayne Fuller forever. I don't like that job, or any other job, all that much. It's just that the money I have won't go far enough. I want a lot of it, Cecily. Someday," she laughed suddenly, "well, someday, maybe I'll have it."

The evening, or what was left of it, went by quickly.

When the bright morning sun awakened me from an uneasy sleep, I was alone in the cottage.

My weekend case was gone.

My bag was gone.

40

The blonde wig was gone.

Fabriana was gone.

I rose, showered. Nervously, I worked with the false lashes until I got them on. I tried not to think too much about the mission ahead. I tried not to consider Fabriana's motives.

She hadn't said she would leave me so early. I had thought there would still be time to talk, question. I supposed that she had wanted to avoid that.

I dressed in the clothes she had left behind. Everything fit perfectly, of course. But I still had a sensation of strangeness. These were not the colors I would have chosen. Not a lime green linen shirt and forest green skirt. Still, within a day or so, I knew I would become accustomed to Fabriana's taste.

When I had completed the makeup, it was almost as if her face looked back at me from the mirror. It gave me an uneasy twinge. I shivered and turned away quickly, warning myself not to become involved with vague and uncomfortable intuitions. I was me, Cecily Harden, and ahead of me there was a test of memory I dreaded.

Would I be able to remember all that Fabriana had told me?

Would I, from Fabriana's description, recognize Mark Winstead, and Dwayne Fuller, and the others?

41

Could I successfully play the part of Fabriana for two weeks?

I tried to concentrate on those practical considerations. Yet most of all I wondered why Fabriana had really asked that I be her on Skeleton Key.

Where would she be for the coming two weeks?

What would she be doing?

Had she really been fearful of her life, only to deny it when I reminded her of what she was asking of me?

Or had she only pretended fear, using it as a weapon against my resistance?

I finally shrugged the questions aside. Soon enough I would have the answers to some of them. And in two weeks I would have the answers to the rest.

Meanwhile, I had to pack Fabriana's bag, pay the motel bill, and then find my way to the marina, where, Fabriana had said, someone would be waiting for her at nine o'clock.

I accomplished the packing, checked the room, and then went to the motel office.

Enrico, the plump, dark desk clerk, smiled at me. "I see your friend got here okay, Miss Harden."

"Yes. She did."

"Gorgeous that blonde hair of hers."

"Isn't it?" I answered.

42

"Always liked blondes," he went on, then added hastily, "like brunettes, too, though."

"My bill?" I asked.

He handed it to me. I fished in Fabriana's purse and found a credit card. I signed her name carefully, glad that the distinctive loops and curlicues were so easy to imitate.

I reminded myself that I must always be careful when I wrote in long hand, and found myself brushing my face as if my long hair had fallen across my cheek. But the long hair was gone now. My head felt strangely light and cool. I must break myself of that habit. I couldn't brush away what wasn't there.

Enrico accepted the signature without question, just as he had accepted me without question. I lingered to chat with him for another moment or two, and then I went out into the hard, bright sunlight.

I followed the directions Fabriana had given me, and easily found my way. I went to the end of the block, turned left, walked another block, and turned right. At the foot of the road, I saw masts and pilings, and a wide arc of aquamarine sea. It was a compelling sight, and I went toward it happily.

The marina itself was small. A covey of rowboats drifted around it. A sleek white motor launch was pulled up alongside. On its hull, in neat black print, was the name

Fabriana had given me.

Caroline I. The launch had been named after Dwayne Fuller's wife, now dead, Fabriana had said, for seven years.

As I drew closer, a man rose up in the launch, and waved his hand in a salute.

I was suddenly breathless.

He climbed onto the marina and came quickly to meet me.

Chapter 3

He was a gracefully moving person, tall and with a whipcord lean body that made it hard to imagine him doing the sedentary work of a writer. He had a shock of wind-ruffled black hair. His face was tanned and angular, with a sturdy jaw and a high, broad forehead. Thick dark brows met in scored lines over the bridge of his straight nose. As he approached me, his narrow lips spread in a casual grin that revealed very white straight teeth. I knew he must be Mark Winstead.

"Hi, Fabriana. Did you have a good time?" he asked, taking the weekend case from my limp grasp.

For just a moment, I froze. I couldn't answer, couldn't move.

Fabriana!

No, I thought. No. I'm Cecily. I must tell this man, tell him at once, that I'm Cecily Harden. The need was so strong, so urgent, that I felt it become words on my tongue.

Then his eyes, eyes as pale as the sand of the Florida beaches, studied me quizzically.

45

"What's the matter?"

I drew on a strength I hadn't known I had. I managed to keep from brushing back a non-existent lock of long hair. I covered breathlessness with a laugh, said, "Hi, Mark. What do you mean 'what's the matter?'"

He gave me another quizzical look, then shrugged. "Did you get your shopping done? And see your friend?"

"I didn't find what I wanted," I answered briefly, covering the fact that here was one small thing Fabriana had overlooked. I had nothing to show for the supposed buying trip. I hurried on, "But I did see my friend all right."

He turned back to the launch. I followed him.

Fabriana's description had been more than adequate. I had been able easily to recognize Mark Winstead from her description of him. But she had not given me a complete picture of the man himself somehow. He had a force, a presence, to which I found myself instantly responding. It made me wary of him.

The wariness grew stronger when he helped me down from the marina. His hand was warm, strong, on mine. The touch was magnetic, at the same time repellent. I was glad when he turned away to busy himself at the controls.

"You don't have to worry about having fallen behind anyway," he said. "We haven't done a thing in the past two days."

"Oh, is that so? Why?"

I hoped that was the sort of thing that Fabriana would have answered. I reminded myself that I must use some of her speech patterns. I must stop thinking of Fabriana but *be* her. But something in me refused that. I was Cecily. I had to remain so.

He raised his voice over the roar of the motor. "You know how it goes sometimes. When I first came down a couple of months ago, Dwayne was in the doldrums. That was because of what happened to Alice, and to Mickey. Both coming so close together. I guess it hit him hard. But he pulled out of it okay. Now . . . I don't know. But there's something in the house . . . maybe just a feeling I have . . . "

Alice . . .

Mickey . . .

For a moment, my mind was a total blank.

I couldn't remember who they were.

Meeting Mark Winstead had unsettled me more than I thought.

He didn't seem to notice my silence. He had begun to uncoil the hawsers from the pilings. He kicked the dock to set the launch adrift, then returned to the controls.

With a sudden roar, the launch cut the sea, leaving a wake of white spume, and rocking the rowboats, as it sped from the protected cove.

Then I remembered. Oh, yes, Fabriana had mentioned Alice Kane. She had been ghost writer for Dwayne Fuller, had been on the Yucatan expedition with him. Several months before, she had been killed in a freak accident the same day that Mickey Hendle, the eighteen-year-old gardener, had drowned. Fabriana had mentioned them both, and their deaths, only in passing. "They're gone. You don't need to know much about them," she had said, and I had accepted that.

Now I wished that she had been more specific. I realized that everyone on Skeleton Key would expect me to have known both Alice and Mickey.

I forced myself to forget them for the moment. Perhaps later I would slowly learn whatever I needed to know about them.

Meanwhile Mark had mentioned that he had a feeling about the house. That interested me. I wanted to know what he meant. But I didn't want to ask him about it directly. I decided that, too, must wait for later.

Now I leaned back in the swivel chair and let the wind blow my new bangs. I blinked the long flashy new eyelashes and felt them brush my cheeks. I began to feel at home in lime green and forest green.

I slid a sideways glance at Mark.

He looked braced, ready for anything, shoulders squared under a rippling white shirt. His legs were muscles, outlined by tight chino trousers. I wondered what he would say if he knew the truth.

Then I found myself wondering what the truth was.

Why did Fabriana want to leave Skeleton Key for two weeks?

Why did she want me there in her place?

It was done, I told myself. No use now to struggle with these doubts. I could spare two weeks out of my life for her. When I met her at the Seaside Motel it would all be finished.

I tried to relax. I didn't want to look ahead, to think of meeting Dwayne Fuller, and his sister Charlotte, and his daughter Karen. I didn't want to try to plan what I would say, how I would act, when I was first exposed to Hank Darrow.

I would be safer, I thought, to allow everything to unfold naturally, not to ask questions, not to comment too much. I must simply wait. I couldn't be Cecily Harden coming to Skeleton Key for the first time. I must be Fabriana returning to her job from Key West after a two day holiday.

I must learn not to flinch when I was called Fabriana. I must learn to be her, to think of myself as her.

But once again I shrank from that thought.

Perhaps I realized, even then, that I must allow my own awareness always to interpose itself between the role and the reality. I must be Fabriana outwardly, but within, I must always be Cecily. That understanding was somehow a comfort to me.

Mark, I realized suddenly, had turned his head, was studying me.

I smiled at him.

He grinned. "A funny thing happened just now, Fab. I mean when you first came walking down to the dock. I thought it was you, and then, for just a minute, I thought I'd made a mistake. I can't explain it."

My heart gave a quick hard jump, and I felt a sudden pulse in my throat.

Mark had seen through the deception, then rejected the truth in favor of what his eyes told him. That was the only way to explain what he had just said.

Aloud I murmured, "That is funny, Mark. Because I *am* me. Obviously."

"Obviously," he agreed. But there was a reservation in his deep quiet voice.

I said quickly, to divert him, "It's a lovely, lovely day, isn't it?"

"As always." He went on, "But you know, I'll be glad when this job is done. I don't much care for the area."

"You don't?"

"No. There's a monotony about it that gets to me after a while. I keep thinking that now that it's autumn the leaves should be changing. There should be wood smoke in the air. Give me New England any time."

I let two heart beats pass before I answered, "I guess it's all what you're used to," hoping that wasn't committing me to some contradiction I didn't know about.

The cliché proved to be safe enough. He didn't bother to answer me.

I thought of the golden leaves I had left behind, the evening chill, the faint haze of smoke rising over the village in early morning. I wished I were back in my cottage. I wished I had never read Fabriana's letter.

But it was too late. The launch skimmed over the still aquamarine surfaces and split gleaming sun reflections, taking me to Skeleton Key. I saw it suddenly. The long flat island, gleaming white, like a jagged pile of bleached bones, rose at the edge of the sea. It had been well named, I thought. A pile of sun-polished wind-scoured bones, surrounded by jagged white teeth that were actually coral reefs.

51

I contained my interest and excitement. It would have been too easy to exclaim at the sight. But I knew that I must not. Fabriana had seen Skeleton Key many many times from this perspective. She wouldn't have cried, "What a weird place! What a good name for it! I want to paint it more than anything in the world!" Fabriana wouldn't react that way, so I dared not either.

The roar of the motor dropped to a slow purr. Ahead I saw buoy markers, one to port and one to starboard. I realized they must mark the narrow channel past reefs I couldn't see.

The buoys rocked at our slow approach. A deep gong rolled through the stillness, then another and another.

Mark was concentrating all his attention on steering, I saw.

When we passed between the buoys, he said, "No matter how many times I do this I always have the feeling that I'm trying to thread a needle."

"It's tricky, I guess."

"I wouldn't want to make the try when the weather goes bad. The channel is very narrow. The reefs are very close to the surface. Even with this boat . . . "

He let his voice trail away.

The buoy gongs sounded once more as the

launch wake rolled them.

Skeleton Key was close now.

I saw the flash of sunlight on glass, and fringes of trees, and long green sloping lawns.

"I wish we didn't keep having these set-backs," Mark said, as he guided the launch close to the small pier. "I really would like to finish up and get away."

"I suppose you would. Still . . . how much longer do you think it will be?" I asked.

Mark's white grin flashed at me. "You're not worried about *your* job, are you, Fab?"

There was implied meaning in his tone. I didn't know what it meant. Perhaps Fabriana would have.

I answered, "I didn't mean that. I was wondering about you."

"I don't know how long the job will last. It all depends on Dwayne. And how things go. And what else develops. You know, with the family . . . " He let that slide as he busied himself tying up the boat.

I realized it was a deliberate elision when, instead of going on with it, he took up my weekend case, asked, "Ready to go up to the house?"

I wasn't ready. I would have much preferred that the trip between Key West and Skeleton Key was much longer. I would have liked to delay my arrival. I would rather have

53

stayed alone with Mark.

But I climbed out of the launch, accepting the hand up that he offered me.

Again, at the touch of his callused palm, I felt a strange warmth. I gained my feet on the pier, quickly turned away from him. I was aware of the quizzical look he gave me.

I decided right then that I must be very careful with him. I would have to see a lot of him, of course, because we would be working together. Fabriana had told me that he would do the rough draft writing, and that I would be typing for him, as well as for Dwayne. But I must remember to be careful. I knew that Mark sensed a strangeness in me, a certain difference. A certain bewilderment peered at me occasionally from his pale eyes. I supposed, without knowing why, that he could be a truly dangerous opponent. I wished that Fabriana had told me more about him than she had.

He said, "I think that two days off did you a lot of good, Fab."

"Yes," I agreed.

"What happened to you anyhow?"

"Nothing special." I went on quickly, "And thanks for coming in to pick me up."

I went up the path between rows of white shells, taking my first steps on Skeleton Key. I didn't know then that I would wish for the

54

rest of my life that I had never gone there, wish that first step had never been taken.

Stately palms, laden with dark brown coconuts, swayed overhead. An emerald green lawn, aglitter under sprinklers, spread up a slight slope, on which the long narrow house was sprawled. It was built of salt-bleached cedar, a pale gleaming silvery gray against the sharp blue of the sky, and the hard white of the coral ridge, and the lush green of vegetation.

It was made in a low rectangle. A center building with dining room, living room, and study, was linked by wings, all containing bedrooms or offices, each of them with doors that opened into the two inner patios.

Fabriana had been insistent that I study the floor plans she had drawn for me. Now I was glad that I had.

I didn't dare examine the place too openly. I was supposed to know it, having lived there for a year.

I didn't dare allow myself to be struck dumb by the sight of it, stand and stare, sensing some cold and awful and ugly aura reaching out for me through the sharp brightness of the sun.

I said hastily, "Whenever you want to get to work, just say so, Mark."

"Thanks. But I doubt that I'll have anything for you today, Fab. Dwayne might though. The mail maybe. He'll tell you."

"I'll check with him."

Mark grinned. "You better. He's been wandering around here the past two days like a bear that's lost his cub. Maybe you can restore him to humor."

"I can try," I said lightly.

Mark opened the tall wooden gate, swung it back.

I passed before him with confidence. I knew this was the patio. The red and orange striped umbrellas and matching chaise longues and upright chairs were exactly as I had imagined them when Fabriana told me about them.

The long beautiful pool glittered like a blue mirror in the sun.

I stopped suddenly.

A girl rose up from a plum-colored towel, shaking golden curls back from her face.

She wore a tiny lavender bikini bra, and minuscule briefs to match. Her skin was a dark tan, her eyes a deep cool blue. She was about twenty-four. Even when she smiled, the lines of discontent that bracketed her mouth were noticeable. She must be, I knew by Fabriana's description, Dwayne's daughter, Karen Fuller.

"Back to Skeleton Key, are you, Fabriana?" she said in a thin, light voice.

I waited, smiling faintly.

"I guess I've lost my bet," Karen went on, with a quick look at Mark.

"Your bet?" I repeated.

"Oh, I'm just kidding. I bet Hank that we'd never see you again."

"Me?" I fluttered my lashes, restraining the impulse to sweep from my cheek a wing of hair no longer there. "Why on earth would I do that, Karen? I have a good job here. Don't you think I know that?"

"Oh, I know you know it," she smiled. "My goodness, yes, no flies on you, Fabriana. I just thought, after what happened, that you'd decide there were good jobs elsewhere, too."

I let my faint smile fade, trying to conceal the bewilderment I felt. How had Karen known that Fabriana didn't want to come back to Skeleton Key?

Obviously Karen accepted me as Fabriana. But she had thought Fabriana wouldn't return. I wondered why.

I said, "Anyhow, I would have said I was leaving if that was what I planned to do."

"Never mind," Karen said. "I lost, the way I always lose."

She lowered herself to her plum-colored towel. She put her hands over her eyes, then said from behind them, "Dad's been wearing out the raffia, waiting for you to get back,

Fabriana. Why don't you go in and put the good guy out of his misery. Or at least out of that part of it?"

I answered, "Oh, does he need me? Then I'd better hurry."

"Need you?" Karen's chuckle was malicious. "Oh, I doubt that. Let's just say he's learned that he can't do without you. And can't do with you either." Her bitter voice trailed away, on "As if you didn't know."

Mark cut in, "Where's Hank?"

"Diddling with the sprinklers. Somebody's got to do something about the gardens. Even with Mickey gone, things grow, you know. It's getting absolutely tacky. My father won't listen when I tell him we need a new gardener. He just can't be bothered. So . . . "

I was more than relieved that I had passed a second test. Karen had plainly accepted me without question as Fabriana. My relief, though, was tempered with the recognition that Karen didn't like Fabriana. I wondered why.

Mark and I passed from the pool patio through a narrow wooden gate set in a low stucco dividing wall and onto the second patio. Here lush vegetation grew in huge wooden tubs: orange birds of paradise and white Venus traps, and thick trumpets. There was a stone figure set among them. It was about my own height, scarred and pitted with time. I didn't dare cross the terrazzo to give it a close look. But I wished I could. I promised myself that I would study it soon. Fabriana had mentioned it, said it was an Indian, carved I didn't remember how many years before, in Yucatan somewhere. I suddenly couldn't remember the name she had told me. I hoped it wouldn't matter. Soon, though, I learned that the Indian's name *did* matter. I know now that I shall never forget it.

"I forgot to tell you," Mark was saying. "Don't get upset when you don't find the rough draft in your room. I hope you don't mind that I went in to get it. I took it back to do the last chapter over again. I'll hand it over as soon as you need it."

I thanked him, hoping my disappointment didn't show too much. It had been from reading the rough draft of Dwayne Fuller's book that I expected to get many of the details of Fabriana's work, and to orient myself in it quickly.

Mark opened an ornately carved wooden door.

From the end of the long, tiled hallway, I heard a voice call, "Fabriana, is that you? I've been waiting. I'm glad you're back. Come and have a late coffee breakfast with me."

It was, it must be, Dwayne Fuller.

But something in his voice — anxiety, affection, and concern — surprised me. Fabriana hadn't prepared me for that.

Just as her description of him, as accurate as it had been, had not prepared me for the sight of him.

Mark said, "Let me take your weekend case to your room for you," and slid it from my suddenly damp fingers.

I nodded my thanks, hesitated, then went toward the shadowy figure that stood waiting for me in the wide arch.

Dwayne was about fifty-five, a tall, heavy-shouldered man, with pale blue eyes, and faded blond hair cut very short. His face was mahogany brown, criss-crossed with smile lines and frown lines. His full mouth was bracketed by permanent creases. He wore dark linen trousers, a dark shirt, open at the throat. He smiled. "How did you make out in Key West?"

"It was fine," I said. "I'm glad I could go."

"Any time you want to, just say the word. I never realized, until you left, that it's so terribly isolated here. I guess I'm so used to jungles I never stopped to think of how it must seem to a young girl like you."

He slid a big hand under my elbow, guided me into the sun-filled room behind him.

I felt as if I had been there before. The portrait that covered one narrow wall was of Caroline Fuller. The huge window looked out on the small patio, and through it I glimpsed the stone Indian figure I had seen from a distance outside.

"Meet your girl friend all right?" Dwayne was asking.

"Sure," I told him, remembering to use Fabriana's speech mannerism.

"Get her problems solved for her?" he grinned.

"I hope so," I answered. I took the seat he had pulled out for me, my eyes straying around the room once more.

The furniture was old, highly polished and carved. The raffia rug was a pale green that seemed to bring the out-of-doors inside. It was a nice place, a quiet one. I could feel at home in it. I remembered, though, that Fabriana had said, "The whole house is full of a lot of old junk."

"I'm afraid we didn't get anything done while you were away, Fabriana. I suppose Mark told you."

I nodded noncommittally.

"Maybe, now that you're back . . ." Dwayne poured coffee for me from a big silver urn. He set the cup before me, and passed me the sugar and cream.

61

I almost refused them since I had become accustomed to taking my coffee black. But then I remembered that Fabriana liked sweet things, creamy things. I helped myself, accepted a slice of toast and spread it liberally with marmalade. I supposed I could change a few of my eating habits for just two weeks.

"Anyhow, now we can get down to it," Dwayne was saying. "I guess everybody hits a slump once in a while, but it's time I got over it. Oh, and I've a nice fat stack of mail for you. Really, the way these things accumulate, I'd sooner do a dig. I know where I am when I'm in the jungle. I just don't like paper work, I guess." His grin spread across his mahogany brown face. "And I guess I've told you that a thousand times, too."

I smiled, said, "Sure you have. But that's what I'm here for. To do the paper work. Or as much of it as I can."

"Well, it won't take you long, if I know you."

I heard the tap of heels in the tiled hall. I was glad of any interruption. What did Fabriana talk about with Dwayne? How did she treat him? How did she feel about him?

There was just too much I didn't know, too much I didn't understand.

I didn't see how Mark, and Karen, and

Dwayne, hadn't realized that they were being deceived.

I sensed, from the look in Dwayne's eyes, from a certain timbre in his voice, that he was expecting something from me. From Fabriana. I didn't know quite what. I had the feeling that Fabriana had not told me all that I needed to be told about herself and Dwayne.

Now the sound of the heels came closer.

I had to pass another test.

A tall, blonde woman came into the bright room. The hard white light from outdoors crossed her face. Small lines and shadows and creases had sudden prominence. She was a pretty woman in her mid-forties, nicely built and graceful in her movements.

This was Charlotte Fuller, I knew, just as Fabriana had described her. "Pretty once, but getting old now. Something of a kook, our Charlotte. Don't worry about her. Just ignore her. She can be a bore, if she wants to." Those had been Fabriana's words.

Charlotte wore a white sharkskin pants suit, and long, dangling earrings, and plenty of makeup. She didn't look like a bore to me. Her blue eyes were very bright, very direct.

I said, "Good morning, Charlotte," and waited breathlessly.

"When did you get back, Fabriana?"

It was all right. I could breathe again.

"Just now," I told her.

Charlotte took a seat at the table. She waved away the toast Dwayne offered her. She accepted steaming black coffee. She concentrated on drinking it. When she had emptied the cup, she passed it back to Dwayne for a refill. Then she smiled coolly at me, and asked, "Now, Fabriana, suppose you tell us just what this is all about?"

Chapter 4

I sat very still, hands holding my coffee cup, aware of the delicate texture of the porcelain, at the same time that I was aware of Charlotte's direct blue gaze.

It seemed to me that the air in the room was suddenly gone.

The sun's brightness and the sea's murmur seemed to disappear.

I hoped that my face remained pleasantly impassive. I hoped that I was successfully concealing the flare of panic that shook me. I took a careful sip of coffee, raised my brows and looked at Charlotte. Without thinking of it, I knew that was exactly how Fabriana would have responded.

I knew I was right when Charlotte said, "Well, you must admit, Fabriana, it is very odd. You've been with us for a year. You've never mentioned friends, or family. We all assumed that you must be alone in the world. And now, very suddenly, without an explanation, you announced that you wanted a couple of days off for shopping, and to see a friend of yours in Key West." Charlotte paused, then chuckled. "It *was* a girl friend, wasn't it?"

"Of course," I answered, and added, very gently, as I knew Fabriana would, "but what I do on my own time is my own business, I think."

Charlotte's direct blue gaze faltered. She said, "You told us that she was in trouble of some sort."

"Yes." I hesitated. Then, "But it's her affair, you know, and not mine to discuss. So, if you'll forgive me, I won't. However, if you feel that you must know her name . . . "

Dwayne cut in sharply, "Nonsense, Fabriana. Her name, her trouble, are certainly not our concern." He turned his narrowed eyes on Charlotte. "I can't understand why you'd question Fabriana like this."

Charlotte said bleakly, "I'm just looking after you, Dwayne, and you *are* my concern." Suddenly she chuckled. "I fear Fabriana takes my heavy attempt at teasing more seriously than it's intended."

It had been heavy, but certainly not teasing. However, I didn't intend to challenge her. I was relieved when Karen and Mark came in together, followed by a tall, blond man. Their entrance created just the diversion I needed.

The blond man was Hank Darrow, Dwayne's photographer, of course. His hair was short, curly, and fell over his green eyes, giving his bronzed, rather mature face a sculptured but oddly boyish look. He wore white shorts, that showed muscled legs, and a brown shirt. I thought him to be about twenty-eight. Fabriana hadn't told me his age.

Now he gave me a quick look, grinned, "Karen and Charlotte were both wrong then. So you did get back after all."

"Of course," I murmured. "And I still don't know why anybody would have thought I mightn't."

"I told them you were a good sport," Hank crowed. He turned to the others. "I did, didn't I?"

Nobody answered him.

Karen seated herself, and Mark and Hank took chairs on either side of her. She looked pointedly at the coffee urn. Hank quickly served her. She thanked him with a jerk of her head. There was a striking resemblance between her and the portrait of her mother that hung on the wall behind her.

I found myself wondering if she deliberately heightened the natural resemblance. She wore her hair the same way, and there was something about her mouth, the corners compressed, that appeared to mock her mother's faint smile.

The sudden silence seemed to prolong itself. It frightened me. I didn't know what to say, what Fabriana had spoken about to these people whom she had known for a year, except for Mark, whom she had known only for two months. It hadn't seemed important the night before when Fabriana was briefing me. Now it was terribly important.

Charlotte said suddenly, "Oh, Dwayne, I'll be so glad when the book is finished. I do wish you'd hurry it up."

He shrugged. "You know these things take time. I can't force the research to go faster than I can do it. I can't make people answer my queries in a hurry just by asking them to." He paused. Then, "And there's no hurry. At least, speaking for myself, there's no hurry. I'm not ready to begin to think about another dig yet, so . . . "

Charlotte's pretty face suddenly showed deeper creases. Her blue eyes looked less bright. She passed a slim hand through her hair, said, "You think you're clever, pretending that you don't know what I'm talking about. But you *do* know. It's Mayeroni. I won't feel right again, not until that manuscript is out of this house and forgotten. I just won't sleep soundly until I know you're finished with it."

I recognized the name the moment I heard

it. Mayeroni. My eyes involuntarily went to the window. Beyond it, in the small patio, I could see the carved Indian figure. He was Mayeroni. From the jungles of Yucatan. He had something to do with Dwayne's expedition, with a part of the book.

Dwayne regarded Charlotte impatiently. "I hope you're not going to start that again. Ever since the night we found Mayeroni, and the old men told us that story, you've been tormenting me with your superstitions. And the worst is, they aren't even *your* superstitions. You heard what the old ones said, and you wouldn't let it go."

"I know what I heard."

"If you can't listen to a legend and identify it, then you mustn't involve yourself in it," he retorted.

"I'm not the one starting it. You are," she answered. She turned, looked at me. "You feel it, too, don't you? You know what I mean, don't you? Fabriana, tell us all the truth, after what happened, isn't that why you wanted a few days away? Because of Mayeroni?"

I hesitated, not knowing what to say. I didn't know what she was talking about. Fabriana had not prepared me for any of this.

But Hank cut in, "Your trouble, Charlotte, is that you just don't have enough to do.

69

You're a young and active woman, with more time on your hands than you need."

She flashed him a look of gratitude at the compliment, and preened briefly. Then she said, "Running this house is a full-time occupation, as you well know. If it weren't for me, none of you would be properly fed. Our dear little Rosa is willing enough, I dare say. But not very bright. Or would you settle for chili for breakfast, tamales for lunch, and chili again for dinner?"

"I would settle for anything," Dwayne retorted, "anything that brought peace to this house, and stopped this foolish quibbling."

Charlotte rose. She said, very deliberately, "I think I'd better see Rosa now about the menu for the rest of the week." She started from the room, then turned back to fire a parting shot at Dwayne. "I think, my dear brother, that if you spent less time lingering over coffee, and other diversions, you might get more work done."

He ignored that, and her departure. He turned a wry smile on me.

I finished the last of my coffee, put down my cup. "I think I'll change and see about your mail now, Dwayne." I glanced at Mark. "And if you don't need the manuscript any more . . ."

He rose immediately. "I'll go with you

70

and hand it over."

"You mustn't let Charlotte get you down," Dwayne told me. "She means well. It's just her nerves. And I suppose I don't appreciate all she does for me."

Karen uttered a bitter chuckle. "All she does for you! She ought to be glad to be here with us, thankful that she has a beautiful home, a place to belong, an interest in her life. If it weren't for us, she'd just be another spinster, living all alone, and drinking her three before-dinner martinis to convince herself that she isn't. If mother were here, Charlotte wouldn't have a look-in."

Dwayne plainly winced. Then he said steadily, "Karen, Charlotte has been very good to us. Where would we be without her?"

"I could do the little that she does," Karen snapped. "And do it better, and without expecting no end of applause for it, too. If it weren't for her . . . "

Once again, Hank cut in. He said, "There you go, Karen. Implying that I'm not interest enough for you."

"Oh, you," she scoffed, but smiled at him.

"There now, that's much better," he was saying, as I left the room with Mark.

I managed to drop back, to allow him to go ahead, unconsciously leading the way for me. It was easier than struggling to remember

71

what Fabriana had told me about the rest of the house. And safer, too. Had I been alone, I would have been able to make an error in finding my way, but not with Mark as witness.

"I suppose you're used to the way they go on," he said quietly. "But I'm not. I don't like it."

I didn't answer him. I didn't like it either. I neither understood nor cared about the cross currents that shook the family.

"Are you still concerned about your friend?" Mark asked.

"I suppose I am. A little."

Yes. I was concerned. Where was Fabriana now? What was she doing? I found myself remembering something Charlotte had said. An odd allusion to things that had happened. I wished I knew what she had meant. I couldn't think of a way of asking Mark.

"If I could help . . . " he was offering.

"I think not. But thank you."

"For nothing," he smiled with a flash of white teeth.

He had paused at the end of the tiled corridor. Now he opened the carved doors, and we stepped out onto the small patio again.

Mayeroni stood there, arms spread wide, in a spotlight of brilliant yellow sun. Heat seemed to shimmer around him.

I murmured, "It's odd. I think that Charlotte is really afraid of him. I wonder why."

"Some people are more prone to superstition than others, maybe." Mark stopped before Mayeroni, and I stopped with him, transfixed by shock that I hoped didn't show.

The Indian's face was malevolent. His mouth was open, lips spread in an awful grin. The carved eyes were deep and sightless, yet seemed to stare into my very heart, warning me of a danger I didn't yet perceive.

"He's not a pretty sight," Mark said. "Maybe that's why, when she first saw him, and heard the story, he hit her that way. Then that business with Alice, and Mickey, must have unsettled her. And that business last week . . . "

I held my breath, hoping he would go on, give me a clue to what he was talking about.

But he had stopped. When he continued, he said, "I wonder what you think about it, Fab. You say so little."

I shrugged.

He smiled faintly. "I don't see you going hysterical over a bit of mischievous intrusion, nor blaming it on an old, long-dead Indian wizard."

"I'm not inclined to think in those terms," I answered.

He led me away from Mayeroni, for which I

73

was glad, and then along the path that ran beside the wing. He stopped before a door, opened it. "Go in. I'll get the script for you right away."

I nodded, took three steps, and paused to look at the azure sky until Mark had gone to a room four doors away and disappeared inside.

Only then did I go into the room he had indicated to me. The weekend case was there. I paused to look around.

It was certainly Fabriana's room.

Her mark was upon it.

For an instant I remembered the room we had shared when we were growing up together.

The litter of belongings that lay wherever Fabriana had dropped them. A pink ribbon on the table top, a pair of sun glasses on the desk. Her own twin bed, and mine, too, awash with discarded blouses . . .

Now, years later, it was exactly the same. I saw that Fabriana still enjoyed living with a certain disorder.

The empty dress boxes amid a crumple of tissue paper took up a wide part of the tan rug. A pile of silk scarves lay on the desk next to the typewriter. A pair of pink slacks hung over an orange easy chair. The clash of colors made me wince. The first thing I did was take up the pants, put them on a hanger, and slip them into the clothes closet. Then I went back to studying the room. I knew I would have to set it to rights. I simply couldn't live for two weeks, nor think for two minutes, confined to such a mess.

The orange drapes framed a wide floor-to-ceiling window. It opened outward, I discovered, onto a path that led into the grounds. Beyond them I saw a narrow rim of aquamarine sea.

My hand itched for a paint brush. It would have been pleasant to have an easel now. To work. To forget my disquieting thoughts.

Why had Fabriana wanted me to come to Skeleton Key in her place?

Had she been frightened by what Mark called those "mischievous intrusions?"

Had she really thought herself in danger and sought my help to escape it?

Or had she, as she said later, simply wanted time off to spend with a fascinating man?

How could I find out?

How could I stay here for two weeks, pretending to be Fabriana? Why had I promised I would do it?

But it was too late then to be asking myself such questions. I was here. I must make the best of it. And, I admitted to myself, it was not unlike Fabriana to have begged me into this adventure simply to free herself for some time off. Still, somehow or other, I didn't quite believe her.

There had been something quite real about her feverish insistence. Even when she abandoned it, it had seemed quite real.

I sighed. All in good time. Eventually I would figure it out, I supposed. I would understand. The pieces of the puzzle would fall into place and I would wonder what had bewildered me so before. Meanwhile, I had to attend to the business at hand.

I was folding away the silk scarves when Mark tapped at the door.

I called to him, and he came in.

His pale eyes narrowed. He laughed. "Are you turning over a new leaf?"

"New leaf?"

"Rosa will think she's lost if she doesn't have to wade through your junk just to get into this room when she comes in to clean."

I winced. There was my first serious mistake. Fabriana was not neat, and never had been. Mark had been in this room, knew that. He was teasing me, his quizzical eyes more amused than suspicious. Still it had been a mistake.

"I'm taken by these spells," I said lightly. "Every once in a while I can't stand myself, and do something about it. Within a couple of weeks it'll all be back to normal, I suppose."

"And I thought you didn't mind that whirlwind going through your things because you couldn't tell the difference anyway."

The whirlwind in my things . . . the mischievous intrusion . . . I understood then. Someone, Charlotte insisted that it must have been the dead Indian, the old stone Indian in the patio, Mayeroni, had been into Fabriana's room, created more disorder than had already been there.

"A girl always knows, no matter how messy she is," I retorted, "when strange hands have disturbed her clothes."

"I guess so. How about when strange hands put ground glass in her orange juice?"

I gave him a startled look.

He said, "Rosa told me about it. I don't know why you thought it had to be a big secret."

I shrugged.

"You don't want to discuss it, is that it?"

"There's nothing to discuss."

He looked at me for a moment, then held out the thick sheaf of yellow manuscript paper.

I reminded myself that I must be careful. I took it from him, dropped it casually onto the scarves near the typewriter. It tipped, and slid, and a few yellow sheets drifted down to settle on the rug.

Mark took that as a matter of course.

He bent to gather the pages. He pulled the scarves off the desk and re-settled the manuscript.

I knew that I had recouped. Fabriana's characteristics were confirmed for him.

I didn't allow myself to show the relief I felt.

I said, "Oh, sorry. Thanks. No disrespect to your work intended."

"None taken," he grinned.

"Why do you really think Dwayne's so stalled on the book?" I asked. The moment the words were out, I wished them unsaid. It might be that Fabriana had already asked the same question at some time or other. It might be that Fabriana was supposed to know more about it than Mark. After all, I had no real picture of what was going on in the house, nor what was in the manuscript yet. Fabriana had been feverishly vague on so many things, I realized now.

But Mark didn't seem to take the question amiss. "What I said before, coming over, he has things on his mind. They're distractions. Are you getting anxious about it? Like Charlotte?"

"No. Not really."

"I suppose I'm the only one around here that has any reason to be in a hurry."

"You?"

"Of course. When the job is done I can take off. I could anyhow, I suppose, but I promised Dwayne I'd do it when Alice died, and I don't want to let him down."

"What about his contract for the book?"

"He can get another extension just like the last time." Mark paused. Then, "What about you though?"

"Me?"

"Will you stay around once the job is done?"

"I suppose so. If Dwayne needs me . . . "

Mark's dark eyes seemed to narrow. He said quietly, "Fab, what do you want out of life?"

I very nearly gave my own answer. I almost said, Why, I want love. What else is there to want? But I caught the words back, hesitating carefully, and then said, "Oh, the same things everybody wants, Mark. You know. A lot of fun. Money maybe. To have happiness."

"You think Skeleton Key is the place to find fun, and money, and happiness?"

Still speaking for Fabriana, I answered, "If it isn't then I'll leave."

It was his turn to hesitate. He studied me. At last he said, "Of course. Why not?"

It was ten-thirty that evening.

I returned to my room, and closed the door

behind me with a deep, relieved sigh.

The strain of pretense had tired me more than I would have thought possible.

I thought with longing of my small cottage, the whisper of golden maple leaves dancing along the slate roof, the misty blue of a cool autumn twilight.

How I wished I had thrown the letter from Fabriana away unread. It began to seem like Pandora's box to me. I couldn't imagine what might come out of it.

I had allowed Fabriana to draw me into a situation that was so odd, fraught with hints of complications I didn't understand. I found myself uneasily adrift in them, unable even to sort out my impressions.

And I was uneasily aware that successful deception for one day didn't mean successful deception for two weeks.

Why hadn't Fabriana told me where I could reach her if I needed to?

Why hadn't I insisted?

There had been, during the day, no time to read the manuscript.

Mark had no sooner left me to my straightening up than Dwayne had appeared. He carried with him a stack of mail. He had insisted that there was no urgency about attending to it, and had lingered, as if unwilling to leave me, until I sat down at the desk.

It took me the better part of the day to answer the letters, to write the requests for information he had directed to several universities both in the United States and in various South American countries.

By afternoon, when I had finished, Dwayne returned to insist that I join the rest of the family for a swim, and then drinks.

I felt self-conscious in Fabriana's scarlet bikini but no one seemed to notice that. Dwayne was attentive enough to make me feel a cruel participant in a cruel hoax. In secret expiation, I suppose, I responded to him. Mark was quiet. I imagined that he generally was. Charlotte had forgotten her morning's outburst, it seemed, and beamed on all of us. Hank and Karen bickered like playful lovers.

Later we all had dinner together.

Afterwards I had expected to make my excuses, plead fatigue, and escape to my room. But Karen insisted on an evening of cards. Fabriana, I guessed, must always have joined the others. She was an avid player. I, not nearly as good, thought I had better not refuse. I had struggled, bored and nervous, to do as well as I could, with Dwayne, Karen, and Hank for my partners. Most of the time, Mark lounged on the sofa, reading, and chatting easily with Charlotte.

Fabriana, I knew, would have been annoyed at Karen's chortling victory. I myself was not. I was only glad that the evening was over.

Now, at last, with the day behind me, I stopped thinking of how Fabriana would think, react, feel. I allowed myself the luxury of being myself. I was Cecily Harden, in my own mind, my own skin.

I pushed myself away from the door, and went to the window to close the orange drapes.

Stars hung like jewels over the fringed tops of the palms and palmettos. The moon was a silver eye studying me through the heavy plate glass.

I drew the drapes, then switched on a lamp. The manuscript was on the desk where I had left it.

I undressed quickly, changing to a pink net gown, wishing for my own cotton pajamas. I brushed my short hair and wished I had back the long heavy weight I had allowed Fabriana to shear away.

I was looking forward to reading the manuscript. I thought I might learn enough from it of the background of the expedition to teach me what I must know about Dwayne's work.

I hung my skirt and blouse away in the closet.

Then I turned to look at the heavy carved wardrobe that stood bulking in the corner. One of its doors hung ajar. I hadn't opened or closed it. I had used only the closet.

I wondered what was in it, and why the door was open. When I touched it, I felt a whisper of movement. It was as if a breath of air had whisked past my cheek.

I stepped back, and at the same moment, the wardrobe shifted. It leaned forward slowly, leaned toward me, and then settled.

I cried out, danced back. At the same moment, it came crashing to the floor.

Chapter 5

I lay sprawled where I had fallen, the sound of the crash still echoing through the room in diminishing thunder.

The heavy wardrobe had burst open at every seam, releasing a flood of books and papers.

Shuddering, I struggled to sit up. And that was when I felt pain. It shot through my whole body from some source in my leg where one weighty panel had come to rest.

Gasping, covered with the cold sweat of shock, and still unable to think, I wrenched at it.

The pain worsened. The pale light of the lamp seemed to fade. I felt myself begin to sink into a wavering darkness.

Then there were voices, the pounding of feet outside.

My door burst open.

Dwayne, in pajamas covered by a white robe, raced in. "My God, Fabriana," he cried. "Oh, my God, what happened?"

He knelt beside me, his mahogany-brown

face suddenly tinged with gray, his blue eyes wild.

I tried to speak and couldn't. The pain was paralyzing. The fear, full grown in an instant, was paralyzing, too. But in that instant, even in my confusion, I was certain that Fabriana had neglected to tell me one very important thing. She hadn't said that Dwayne Fuller was in love with her.

It was Mark, appearing silently from the dark of the patio, who said, "Let's get this thing off her, Dwayne. I'm afraid she's been hurt."

Dwayne groaned, "Oh, yes, yes. What's the matter with me?"

The two men grappled with the panel. They strained to ease it away.

As soon as my leg was free the pain lessened. I could breathe again. I struggled to sit up.

Mark said, "Lie still. I'll get ice."

He brushed past the others who had gathered around the door, and vanished into the patio.

Dwayne was near me again. He took my hand. "Wait Fabriana. Rest a minute."

The emotion in his face, voice, hurt me terribly. My deception had led him to expose himself to me, to a stranger. Unwittingly, he had opened the privacy of his feelings to a person who had no right to know them.

How could Fabriana have been so cruel?

Gently I disengaged my hand from him. I sat up carefully. My leg throbbed, reminding me of what had happened.

Charlotte stumbled into the room with Karen and Hank at her heels. She stood over me, her eyes blazing, "Now what is it? How did you manage to accomplish this mess?"

Dwayne cried, "Charlotte, be still!"

I smiled faintly. "I don't know how I accomplished it. But I assure you, it wasn't deliberate. I simply went to the wardrobe to close a door that was hanging open. When I touched it, the whole thing seemed to sway . . ."

I let my voice trail off. I was remembering exactly how it had been. The door ajar . . . My fingers brushing the carved wooden knob . . . The feeling that the whole huge thing had seemed to sway, creating a draft, and then suddenly toppled over.

"But you're not hurt, are you?" Karen asked.

I couldn't detect much real concern in her voice, but her eyes were serious, looking down at me.

"This old stuff," Hank said. "I always thought it would fall apart if you breathed on it hard. And it did."

I got to my feet, Dwayne helping me carefully. Leaning on him, I made my way past the debris, the scattered books, to the bed. I sat down, wincing, as my leg throbbed.

That was when Dwayne said, "Spanish chests don't fall apart. A three-hundred-year-old wardrobe should last another three hundred years."

"And they don't just fall over either," Charlotte cut in stridently. "Don't you realize that? It couldn't possibly have fallen over when Fabriana touched it."

From the doorway there was a rustle of angry movement. Rosa thrust herself into the room. She was dressed in a white ruffled nightgown, over which she had flung a black shawl. She looked like a small, plump angry doll. She came over and stood before me.

"I didn't do it! Whatever happened, it wasn't me! I know what you thought. You always thought it was me that messed up your things. Well, I didn't! You thought it was me that put ground glass in your orange juice. I told you then, I tell you now. It wasn't me! And this, tonight, now, I was asleep in my bed, as a decent person would be. I didn't do this. Don't look at me!"

The mischievous intrusion in Fabriana's room . . .

The ground glass in her orange juice . . .

87

The wardrobe . . .

Now I knew for certain that Fabriana had been truly frightened. And now I knew why. She hadn't wanted to spend two weeks with a man and then return to her job. She had wanted to escape her terror, and leave me in her place.

Intuition told me to unmask myself. It told me to explain that I was Cecily, and not Fabriana. It told me that Dwayne, the others, must immediately know the truth.

I struggled with it briefly, then I smothered it deep and hard. I found that I could not betray Fabriana now, not until I knew the whole truth myself.

What had she done?

Why was she in danger?

"Don't look at me," Rosa was repeating, her dark eyes round with anger, and shining with fear. "I didn't do it!"

I said quietly, "Oh, Rosa, of course you didn't. I never blamed you. Why should you think I did?"

"Because I could feel it," she retorted. "I saw it in your looks. I saw it when you spoke to me."

"I'm sorry. I think you misunderstood me, Rosa. I never blamed you in my mind."

"Of course not," Dwayne said heartily. "Why, she brushed it all aside as if it had never happened. She just didn't take it seriously. Maybe you did, Rosa, but she didn't."

"And now this," Charlotte murmured, drawing her satin robe more tightly around her. "This. And none of you are willing to speak the truth. You all know what it is. You know what happened in this room ten days ago. You know how the glass got into Fabriana's orange juice. You know how that wardrobe came to fall over tonight."

Karen muttered, "Oh, here we go again."

With her white face crumpled into wrinkles, her eyes blazing, Charlotte suddenly looked old. Her voice cracked as she whispered, "You can feign ignorance, all of you can, but you know the truth as well as I do. I knew the truth when I heard it that night, when the old men told us. You knew it then, too. I've warned you and warned you . . ."

Dwayne said sharply, "Charlotte, control yourself. Hysteria won't help."

"What about Alice Kane?" she screamed.

I forced my wandering attention back to what she was saying. Alice Kane, the writer who had been working with Dwayne, until two months before . . . Why was Charlotte mentioning her now?

Dwayne said wearily, "That was a terrible accident, and you know it, Charlotte."

"And Mickey Hendle! I suppose his death

was an accident, too?"

"Of course," Dwayne told her.

"I warned you then, and you all laughed at me. Are you laughing now? Fabriana? What about you? Are you still laughing at me?"

"Oh, leave her alone," Hank cut in. "I don't see the point of your badgering her, and us. Crazy things happen and that's that. Just let it be, Charlotte."

"I agree," Karen said coolly. "This hardly is the time to get on your superstitious horse."

The argument stopped when Mark returned. He carried an icepack wrapped in a green towel.

He gave the others a quick angry look. "I could hear you in the main house." His glance touched Rosa. "Do you think you could make us some coffee?"

She nodded, went out.

He came to lean over me. "I think you should lie down, Fab. Let me get this on your leg. It'll help. Then, in the morning, I'll take you in to the doctor."

"I don't think it's necessary," I protested. "The throbbing is much less. There's nothing there but a bruise."

I was suddenly aware of my flimsy gown. I drew it more tightly around me.

Mark adjusted the icepack just below my knee, bound it with a cord he had brought with him. At his touch I felt a peculiar sense of safety, a sharp sweet heightening of awareness. He must have sensed something of it because he gave me a sharp, pale glance.

Then he looked up. "You could have begun to straighten this mess, Karen."

Dwayne answered, "Charlotte's been busy entertaining us. I suppose we were too busy listening."

Mark grunted. His hands fell away from my knee. He straightened. "Rosa's got coffee ready. Why don't you all have some?" He glanced down at me. "Fab? What about it?"

I nodded thankfully. I thought that a good hot stimulant might do me good.

"I'll get it," Karen offered. But she didn't move. She stood still, staring at the debris of the wardrobe, the shattered panels, the litter of heavy books and paper scattered around it. "I can't understand it though."

Charlotte's voice was low, bitter. "Of course you can. But greed drives all of you. Greed makes you think that you're bigger, safer, stronger, wiser than other men."

"Charlotte . . . " Dwayne began.

"It's true," she went on, "you know it's true. It's the curse of Mayeroni. You violated him, and betrayed him. You brought him here and set him up in the patio as if he were a dead thing, defeated and powerless. Now you know."

The curse of Mayeroni . . .

I saw the stony malevolence in the small face, the mouth turned down, the sightless eyes . . .

I shivered with sudden chill.

But Dwayne sighed in exasperation. "Charlotte, please."

"I ask you again. Why did Alice Kane die? Why did Mickey Hendle die? Why has Fabriana been endangered?"

"And I'll say again that accidents do happen. I agree with Dwayne," Hank said quietly, his bronze face completely without doubt, his green eyes full of assurance.

He, I was certain, believed what he was saying.

"Mayeroni's curse is fact. It's been proven true for centuries in Yucatan. And it's been proven fact right here on Skeleton Key," Charlotte retorted.

She, I was certain, believed what she was saying.

I listened, trying to absorb, to understand.

Alice Kane. Mickey Hendle. Mayeroni.

I hoped that somehow I would soon discover the clues I needed to make sense out of Charlotte's assertion and Hank's denial.

Hank said, "Poor Alice just happened to be under that palm when the shower of coconuts fell. It was one of those once-in-a-generation

92

accidents. And, after all, Alice certainly didn't have anything to do with Mayeroni's treasure. She was only Dwayne's ghost writer. And as for Mickey Hendle, how on earth you can think that he had . . . "

Dwayne interrupted, his voice raw with barely suppressed irritation, "That's enough. Fabriana doesn't want to hear any more of this nonsense and neither do I. Why don't the rest of you go into the main house and get your coffee. And you, Karen, since you offered . . . "

She nodded, went to the door, and looked back for a moment. Her eyes met mine, cold, detached, thoughtful. Then she shrugged and left.

"I'm sorry for you," Charlotte said quietly. "Sorry you won't listen, think. There have been two deaths already. Now this. Do we all have to die? You still refuse to believe me. If you don't stop writing that book, if you don't stop threatening the treasure that Mayeroni guarded, his curse will destroy us all."

The treasure that Mayeroni guarded . . .

The chill of apprehension was on me again. I shivered and Mark glanced down at me.

But Dwayne said wearily, "I've told you a dozen times that there is no treasure in the first place. No treasure. No curse. If you don't believe me, I can't help it."

"The legend holds . . . "

"Never mind." Dwayne smiled at me. "I'm sorry. Just don't pay attention. Karen will be back with your coffee. We'll all calm down, and then we'll clean up the mess in here so you can get some sleep."

Charlotte gave a disgusted gasp and stalked from the room.

Hank grinned, "Take it easy, Fabriana," and followed her out.

Dwayne was obviously waiting for Mark to leave.

Instead, when Mark moved away from me, he went to the shattered wardrobe and squatted down on his heels. He brushed books and papers aside, and ran his fingers over the bits of broken carved wood that had been legs.

"We'll have a good look in the morning," Dwayne told him.

"Let's move it into the workroom now," Mark suggested.

Dwayne glanced at me, hesitated, then agreed.

He and Mark stacked the books and papers against the wall. Then, heaving together, they got the broken wardrobe upright. It wouldn't stand on its own. It leaned forward, toppling until they braced it with their shoulders.

I wished that I had told them to leave it where it had been. I realized suddenly that I wanted to examine it myself. I wanted to look at those shattered legs.

But it was too late. Between them, Dwayne and Mark managed to ease it through the door.

A moment after they left, Rosa came in. She busied herself pouring coffee from a small porcelain pot, added sugar and cream, then handed me a cup.

I thanked her, said, "Rosa, I mean it. I never thought you were responsible for any of this."

"Mayeroni," she told me. "Charlotte knows. I know. But you're different now."

My heart gave a sudden leap.

What had I done?

How had she guessed?

She went on thoughtfully, "I guess it's because you understand. You understand, and you're scared. And being scared makes you different."

"I don't think I believe in Mayeroni," I said carefully.

She gave me a dark reproachful look. "That's what you told me before."

I nodded. I sipped the reviving coffee slowly.

She asked, "Do you want anything else?"

I shook my head.

"Do you want me to stay with you?"

"No, Rosa. But thank you."

She stared at me, the round doll face thoughtful. Then she shrugged. "Yes, you're scared. That's why you're different, I guess."

After giving me another long silent look she left. I knew that somehow, in some way I didn't understand, she had sensed the fact that I was not actually Fabriana. She felt a difference, recognized it, responded to it. I knew that I would have to be very careful with her from then on, if I intended to stay on Skeleton Key.

Alone, I asked myself why the wardrobe had fallen just when it did.

What did Charlotte mean by the Mayeroni treasure? The Mayeroni curse? The Mayeroni myth?

How could what happened tonight have anything to do with that? Or with Alice Kane and Mickey Hendle? And was this what Fabriana had feared?

Had she really sent me to take her place when she believed that her life was in danger? Was I, as her surrogate, to die?

Had she believed that I could solve the mystery of Skeleton Key, and save myself, and her, within the two weeks she had specified?

There were too many questions. Too much had happened since I had left my small cottage, my easel and paints, and flown down to Key West.

I was confused, adrift, lost. I was afraid.

I found myself wondering if that was how Fabriana had felt when she sat down at the desk in this room and wrote the letter on blue stationery that had called me to her.

Dwayne returned alone, silently.

I started when his shadow suddenly fell over me.

He noticed, smiled, "Don't Fabriana. It's only me. I can't bear your being afraid."

I smiled at him. "I'm all right. Really, Dwayne. I am."

"I worry that Charlotte might have gotten you nervy with her foolish talk."

"No." I half-lifted my hand, then let it fall. I had been about to brush back a wing of long hair. I wondered how much time it would take me to break myself of that now useless habit.

His blue eyes were intent, staring into my face, trying, I thought, to see past it, into my mind. He said, "When I heard that crash . . . you don't know . . . And your scream . . . I thought . . . "

A quick pulse began in my throat. I felt suffocated by a wave of embarrassment again. His manner, the look on his face, in his eyes, the tenderness in his voice, was something I couldn't deal with. They were for Fabriana, not for me.

I couldn't bear to stand witness to them.

I didn't know if he had ever declared himself to her. I didn't know what her reaction to him had been.

I smiled faintly, closed my eyes.

He said quietly, "You're exhausted. Forgive me. I must let you rest now."

"Yes," I murmured. "Thank you. I'll be fine by morning, I know."

"Mark thinks you should have your leg x-rayed."

"Oh, no. The ice is helping a lot. It hardly hurts now."

"You're very brave, Fabriana. You've always been."

I smiled again. "Not as brave as you think, Dwayne."

When he had gone, closing the door softly behind him, I managed to sit up. I limped to the desk and got the manuscript. I returned to the bed, lay down, and adjusted the ice-pack that had slipped a little, remembering the touch of Mark's hands when he put it on me.

I dismissed that recollection as something I must not allow myself to dwell on.

The house was so still now that from a long way off I could hear the whisper of the sea, the song of the wind in the tall palms.

How different it was here on Skeleton Key, different from the village I called home. Suddenly I longed for it, for the remembered sense of safety, the orderliness and creativeness of my days there.

"Soon, soon," I told myself. Soon I would be there again.

I sighed, settled myself against the stacked pillows. When I understood what was happening here, I could leave.

I adjusted the lamp, and took up the manuscript, and began to read.

Hours later, with the yellow pages scattered around me, I stared at the orange drapes that covered the big window and wondered at what I had learned.

Chapter 6

Dwayne's book was about the archaeological expedition which he had led into the wild jungles of Yucatan several years before. He had been in search of the site of prehistoric religious ceremonials about which very little was known. He believed he had found them.

Accompanying him on the expedition were Hank Darrow, acting as his photographer, Alice Kane, who helped him take notes at that stage, and Karen and Charlotte. With him also were several guides, servants, and helpers.

There were, so far, only a very few pages devoted to Mayeroni. But in these I found the facts which explained to me Charlotte's hysterical outburst.

Mayeroni had been an Indian priest in prehistoric times, and had officiated at twice yearly sacrificial ceremonies. At each one a virgin princess, dressed in gold-woven cloth and arrayed in golden armlets, bracelets, and necklaces, was flung alive into a bottomless pit that led to an underground river.

The practice had existed for untold generations before Mayeroni became the officiating priest, but it was in his time that it was discovered that marauders had desecrated the holy place in search of accumulated treasure. Mayeroni had laid a curse upon anyone who found the gold and jewels, or anyone who sought it. He had sworn to his ancient gods that those who defiled their altars would die. Dwayne called this curse the Mayeroni myth.

He wrote that he had found no treasure in the place that he thought to be the original location of the ancient sacrifices. Either there had never been such treasure, or it had been removed hundreds of years before.

But I knew that Charlotte believed in the treasure and in the Mayeroni curse. She felt that the expedition had violated the religious ground, and that the treasure was there. She believed in Mayeroni himself as a living presence.

It was on his curse that Charlotte blamed Alice Kane's death, and Mickey Hendle's. On it, too, that she blamed what had happened to Fabriana in the weeks just past. What had happened to me that very night.

I found myself shivering, as if chill from the icepack on my knee had suddenly spread throughout my body. I looked slowly around the room.

Fabriana had been here for a year. She had

lain on this bed, studied these very walls. And she had become afraid.

First she had admitted it. Then denied it.

But now I knew the truth.

She *had* been afraid. Was it the Mayeroni myth that had frightened her? Did she believe that an ancient curse was reaching out to destroy her? To destroy all that lived in the house on Skeleton Key?

The others had laughed at Charlotte's openly expressed fear, but had they made light of it to cover their own terror?

But, at first, Fabriana had said that if I didn't trade places with her she would surely die.

She hadn't told me why she thought so. She hadn't said that someone had been into this very room, disarrayed her belongings in some way that frightened her. She hadn't said that she'd found ground glass in her orange juice.

When I had questioned her she'd claimed that her fear had been make-believe. She'd wanted to spend two weeks with some man, then return to her job. She'd only wanted me to hold her place with Dwayne Fuller for her.

But tonight, my first night here, the wardrobe had fallen. I had evaded death by a hairsbreadth only.

Why had it swayed, then settled, then tipped so heavily toward me?

Mark had insisted that it be removed from the room. Dwayne had immediately concurred.

Was it because neither of them wanted me to look at it, examine it?

Were they afraid of what I would find?

I decided, then, that I would locate the wardrobe in the workroom to which Mark had said he would take it. I would study it for myself. Perhaps I could learn something from it. Perhaps it was man's hands, not the weight of a myth, that menaced me.

I awakened to the sound of footsteps outside my door. I sat up, suddenly aware of an aching in my leg. For a moment, I didn't know where I was, or why. I was startled by my surroundings, the dim orange glow, the trill of distant birds.

Then memory came flooding back.

The lamp burned faintly. Beside it, on the night table, there was the manuscript.

Now I remembered reading it, setting it carefully aside, my mind awhirl with terrifying images . . . the green-shadowed jungle aglow with giant torches . . . flames gleaming on golden ornaments and glittering on polished jewels . . . young, tear-wet faces twisted in final anguish . . . the screams of parrots and monkeys mingling with the screams of the sacrificed . . . Mayeroni, demanding the wrath of his ancient gods to protect the treasures offered to them . . .

I shook away the recollection of my uneasy dreams.

I rose carefully, and found that I could stand.

The voices beyond my door were louder now.

I heard Mark say, "Maybe you should let her sleep longer this morning, Rosa."

"She always wants her coffee now. You know that. I know that. It is always that way. If I don't give it to her she'll be mad at me."

I slipped into my robe, limped to the door and opened it.

Rosa stood on the step, holding a tray. Her lower lip was jutted out. Her dark eyes held a stubborn glint.

I smiled at her. "Oh, Rosa, what a wonderful idea. Just what I need this morning."

"You see," she told Mark.

He grinned at me. "I thought you'd need more rest."

Rosa went past me into the room.

I blinked into the brilliant sunlight. "No, I'm fine, Mark."

"How's the leg?"

"Bruised but unbroken. I can manage quite well, if I favor it just a little."

"I'll leave you to Rosa then. But don't hurry. We won't have much to do, I'm afraid. Dwayne was good and rattled last night. And I don't think he'll be able to settle down to-day."

"Would you want to have coffee with me?" I asked.

"I hoped you'd suggest it," Mark grinned.

"Then come in."

I turned to look at Rosa. "Would it be too much trouble to find an extra cup for Mark?"

She didn't answer. She drew back the drapes, then turned to the table. She snapped a white linen napkin from the tray, revealing coffee and toast, and a tall glass of orange juice. She hustled into the bathroom and returned with an extra cup and saucer.

"No glass in the orange juice," she said quietly. "I strained it. Just to be sure."

"But you shouldn't have," I protested. "Oh, Rosa, nobody ever blamed you for that."

She didn't answer me.

Mark took the chair near the desk.

I limped to one next to it.

Rosa served us both, then asked, "Anything else you want?"

"No, thanks," I told her. "I'm sorry to be so much trouble."

Rosa's brown eyes widened in her plump doll face. "Trouble?"

"I mean your bringing my breakfast here . . ." I stopped. I suddenly realized that Rosa always brought Fabriana breakfast in her room. Rosa's words just beyond the door indicated that. I floundered, trying to recover, "I really could eat with the others, but . . ."

"But you never do," Rosa said. "Always, since you first came, you insisted on breakfast alone."

"I know," I said quickly, "but I've just realized that you have enough work to do without me asking for special service. In the future, I'll . . ."

"I don't mind," Rosa said. "And when you put it like that . . ." Her brown eyes swept me up and down. "Did you get hurt last night?"

"No."

She cocked her head. "Just scared?"

"I suppose."

"Remember Mayeroni," she whispered. "He's here. He's here with us. Not just him, standing in the small patio, with his arms spread. But here in the spirit, too. It has to be Mayeroni." She turned to Mark. "Just like Alice. Like Mickey. That dear sweet boy. That Mickey. What else could it be but Mayeroni? I told you, Mark. You better listen to me. Listen to Charlotte. They all better listen. It's Mayeroni all right." She waddled to the door, looked back. "You, too, Fabriana. You'd better listen, too."

When we were alone, Mark said, "You surprised her, Fab."

I poured coffee for him, for myself, before answering. "I guess I did. But I just never thought . . . it seemed a reasonable routine to me, and then, suddenly, today, I saw that it must be a problem for her to pamper me so."

"It's funny," he said, "what an accident will do. I never heard her speak to you the way she spoke to you this morning."

"Maybe it's because I'd hurt my leg," I suggested.

He studied me, took a sip of coffee, then said, "The way her reaction to you changed . . ."

Fabriana hadn't told me that she and Rosa had never gotten on well. I imagined that I knew why. Fabriana could be sharp with people, curt with servants, could expect too much and forget to show gratitude. I supposed that Rosa had sensed the difference between the two of us, and when I had suggested that Rosa stop serving breakfast in my room that had stressed it. I thought once again that I had better be very careful with her.

Yet I did want to talk to her. She seemed a

simple and direct person. Perhaps through her I could learn more about the deaths of Alice Kane and Mickey Hendle.

I realized suddenly that Mark was watching me.

I said, "Rosa really believes in the Mayeroni myth."

"And what about you?" he demanded.

I knew enough now to be certain that Fabriana had laughed over the old legend, refused to take it seriously in any way. Somehow I couldn't force myself to do that. I shrugged, said, "Mark, I just don't know what to think."

"How about Alice Kane? What was her reaction?" His dark eyes were narrowed watchfully.

I knew that his question wasn't an idle one. I answered honestly, "I don't have any idea what Alice thought."

I considered myself safe in that. It hardly seemed likely that a writer like Alice Kane, or one like Mark himself, would have much time for old superstitions.

"I always wanted to ask you, Fab . . . you knew Alice. What did you think of her?"

"She was talented, interesting, very pleasant," I told him with more assurance than I felt. I couldn't help but wonder why he was asking me about her, just what it was that he was driving at. "Did you ever meet her?" I added as part of my reply.

"Oh, yes, a couple of times. You know how it is in our field. You cross paths here and there. We belonged to the same writers' organization, too."

"Then you probably have some ideas about her yourself."

"Some," he agreed briefly. "But they don't fit in with what I've heard since I've been here. That's why I was curious."

"What do you mean?"

He shrugged. "Little things here and there. Charlotte said that Alice was a troublemaker. From what I knew of Alice I found that hard to believe. And then, Karen has implied several times that it's Alice's fault that Dwayne was so stalled on the book. She was an extremely professional person. At least, I thought she was, from our very few contacts. I've found myself wondering if the family will end up saying the same kinds of things about me. I wouldn't relish that."

"Of course you wouldn't." That seemed a safe enough comment to me. I didn't know what to say about Alice Kane. I went on, to change the subject, "Charlotte was very upset last night. I hope she's all right this morning."

"She seems to believe in the myth, Fab. And it just strikes me wrong. She's not the sort of woman, I would have thought, who'd give herself so completely to superstition. Still . . . there *have* been these strange . . . "

"You sound as if you're beginning to accept the idea yourself, Mark."

"I guess not, Fab. There is always more than one explanation for how things happen, I've found." He drained his cup and rose. "I'd better get to work. I'll see you later, won't I?"

"Of course. I'll stop in Dwayne's office in a few minutes. There might be something he needs me for."

"I doubt if he'll have any work for you," Mark answered.

When he had left me, I showered and dressed. I put on a pink pants suit and pink sandals. I found myself missing my comfortable paint-stained blue jeans. I told myself to stop being childish and tackled my face. The lashes took me longer than my patience would stand for. I finally gave up and settled for liner and shadow, assuring myself that Fabriana couldn't possibly have gone through this routine every morning. Particularly not on those mornings after which she had had her mysterious brushes with either the supernatural or the hidden malice of man.

It was just as I was preparing to leave my room that I suddenly realized how odd it had been that Mark should have asked me so many questions about Alice Kane.

Had he been trying to learn something about her that he thought I might know?

Or had he been checking me?

Did he suspect, after all, that I was not Fabriana herself?

I stood before the portrait, drawn to it for reasons I didn't understand. It hung now part in shadow, part in a ray of light from the glass wall, where Mayeroni stood with spread arms, and evilly turned-down mouth.

Caroline Fuller had been tall, slender, very beautiful. She wore close-fitting suntans, and jungle boots, and her hair was long and golden. Her eyes were a deep blue. Her mouth was narrow, faintly smiling. Her cheekbones were high, with sculptured hollows beneath them.

I found myself wondering how she had died, what had happened in the fullness of her middle thirties, the prime of her life.

"Beautiful, wasn't she?"

I turned, startled.

Karen stood at my shoulder.

She wore light tan trousers, a tan open-necked shirt. Once again I was struck by the remarkable resemblance she had to her mother. And once again I wondered if she deliberately stressed it.

"You're very like her," I said gently.

"Yes," Karen agreed, deepening the smile that was so much like her mother's. "Yes, I am. Everyone says so." The fact obviously pleased her. She went on, "But not in every way, of course." She paused. Then, "I never knew you to admire the portrait before though."

Fabriana, of course, paid very little attention to painting, while I paid more attention to it, perhaps, than I should. I hesitated, then answered, "I've always admired it very much, Karen. I suppose it just never came up though. And just now, as I passed through the dining room, I had the feeling that she was looking at me. It's a difficult effect to achieve. I imagine it is, anyhow."

Karen's smile had turned bitter. "It's an effect all right. And just that. No more. She . . . she never really looked at anybody. Only in the mirror at herself. And, of course, at my father. They had this thing between them. It didn't leave room for anyone else."

I was afraid to make any comment. I had no idea of how much Karen had spoken to Fabriana about her mother. Almost immediately I found out.

Karen was staring at me. She said, "That's funny. I've never said anything like that to anybody. You're a lot easier to talk to than you've ever been."

"I'm sorry if I haven't been easy to talk to before," I told her.

"Maybe I'm not so easy myself." Karen gave the portrait another look, then deliberately turned her back on it. She asked, "Is your leg all right this morning?"

"Oh, yes. Just a bit bruised. I've almost forgotten about it."

"Almost forgotten what happened?"

I shrugged.

She laughed softly. "My father will be very pleased and very relieved."

I saw no reason to answer that.

"It could have been much worse," she told me. "I guess you realize that, Fabriana."

"I suppose so. So there's no use worrying about it." I made myself grin. "Look, Karen, you don't believe in all that nonsense, do you?"

"Me?" Karen laughed. "No, of course not. How could I believe in anything that square? I leave that stuff to the old biddies like Charlotte."

"I doubt she'd appreciate being called an old biddy."

Karen shrugged her slim shoulders. "Never mind her appreciation. Maybe she is my aunt, but she can be an awful pain in the neck. You know how she keeps trying to push me off on Hank. I hate that. Who I marry is my business. When I'm ready to make up my mind I will. I don't see why she's got to keep nagging at me about it. Maybe she just wants to keep my father's photographer in the family. Or maybe she just wants to get rid of me. But whatever it is, I don't like it."

"I know she means well," I said. "And you do like Hank, don't you?"

"Sure. Why not? I have to do something around here, don't I? Amusing myself with Hank is something."

"Is that really all it is?"

"Hank . . . " She let her voice dismiss him. She said, "They come in threes, Fabriana."

"What does?" But my question was a formality only. I knew just what she would say. My attention sharpened even more.

"Accidents," she said softly. "They come in threes. And you've had three, haven't you?"

There was an odd note of warning in her tone. I wondered if it was deliberate.

I said lightly, "I'm not superstitious, Karen. Maybe because I'm not an old biddy."

"No," she said, giving me a long cool look. "No, Fabriana, you're certainly not that."

Without another word, she turned and left me.

The encounter had left me uneasy, but I was determined to find the workroom Mark had mentioned the night before, determined

114

to examine the broken wardrobe. I went into the tiled hall, and through the carved doors into the small patio.

Mayeroni stood in clear sharp shadow. I hurried past him. There was a low wooden gate in the wall that led outside. I hurried through it, and immediately knew I had guessed right. I hurried into the stucco shed.

The wardrobe was tilted back against the wall, its doors broken on their hinges and sagging. Its panels were shattered in two places. The panel that had split away and fallen on my leg was standing nearby.

I knelt, conscious suddenly of my bruises, to study the four-inch carved legs that had supported the wardrobe. The two front ones were splintered. I bent closer, peering at them. There was a jagged torn place on each one. But there was also a smooth, plainly cut-through area.

I drew my breath in harshly. The piece was extremely heavy. If the front legs had been carefully cut part way through, the wardrobe would have toppled forward at the lightest touch.

Mischief explained the disturbance of Fabriana's room.

Accident explained ground glass in her orange juice.

But this was a deliberate attempt at murder.

Chill wrapped me in cold fingers.

Fabriana's terror had been real. I was certain of that now.

My mind went back to the night before. We had all been in the living room. Karen and Hank had partnered Dwayne and me at bridge. She had been dummy several times. So had Hank. Dwayne had been dummy once. They had each left the room for a little while. Karen to stretch her legs, Hank to get a fresh pack of cigarettes, Dwayne to refill our drinks. Mark had read, chatted desultorily with Charlotte; then they had left us to go to sleep, they had said.

Each of them had had time, if he moved quickly, to tamper with the wardrobe.

But why, why would any of them want Fabriana to die?

There was a sound behind me.

My heart began to beat quickly. I got to my feet awkwardly, aware of the sudden shadow.

Hank asked, "Are you looking for something, Fabriana?" and grinned.

Chapter 7

I tried to conceal the shock of fright by grinning back at him, asking lightly, "Do you have to creep up on people like that?"

He seemed aggrieved. "I wasn't creeping. I wear these sandals because they're comfortable. I can't help it if they don't make any noise. I think you're just nervy this morning."

"You're forgiven."

"But what were you looking for?"

"I don't know," I told him, determined not to mention what I'd found, to distract him from looking at the wardrobe for himself.

But he didn't go toward it. He moved out of the shed, and into the sunlight. He squinted up at the sky. "Listen, you didn't take Charlotte's nonsense seriously, did you?"

"No. But it was a funny thing to happen."

Still looking up at the sky, he said, "You've got nerves of steel. We all know that, Fabriana. You can't be shaken by small things."

"That wardrobe is not a small thing."

"Oh, but accidents do happen. You've said so yourself more times than I can count."

Hank could, I saw, be very persuasive when he wanted to be. I wondered why he wanted to be now.

Had he used a small saw on the wardrobe?

Was he behind the attempt on my life?

Was it he who Fabriana feared?

"That's what we've all so much admired about you," he went on. "Those nerves of steel of yours. That," his eyes swept me in a quick green look full of implication, "plus certain other things."

I could almost have laughed. Perhaps he was thinking of Fabriana, as he knew her. He was certainly not thinking of the real me. I could hardly be said to have nerves of steel. I simply did what had to be done. Never mind how I felt about it. It had been another one of those differences between Fabriana and me. She had always let her terrors rule her. I was never able to.

I started for the gate, but Hank took my hand.

"Wait," he said. "Tell me, Fabriana. Why were you looking at the wardrobe?"

"Because I wondered why it fell over on me," I said tartly. "Anybody with good sense would."

"And do you know why now?"

"No," I lied. "And I suppose I won't ever know either."

He dropped my hand. "Oh, there's probably just nothing to know."

I grinned, "I expect you're right, Hank," but wondered if I were imagining only the faint traces of relief I thought I saw in his bronzed face.

We separated then.

As I walked through the patio alone I thought about the wardrobe. Now I knew that it had been tampered with. An attack on my life was made to appear accidental.

My first night on Skeleton Key had given me evidence of what Fabriana feared, then denied. It proved to me that she had offered me as a sacrifice on the altar of her terror.

But why had she done it?

Who had she so feared?

Walking through the hot bright sunlight, I shivered.

Who? Why?

Until I learned the answers to these questions, I knew I would never be safe. Fabriana would never be safe.

I suddenly wondered if I could manage to last out the two weeks that I had promised her. I wished I knew where she was, how I could find her.

"I don't know," Dwayne said. He leaned back in his padded swivel chair, his heavy shoulders sagging. He looked crisp and fresh in a blue, open-necked shirt and dark blue trousers. But his eyes, firmly fixed on the distant horizon, were troubled. "I just can't settle down, Fabriana. I can't think."

There was a scatter of crumpled white sheets around the floor at his feet. His desk was covered with stacks of books, sheaves of periodicals, and regiments of sharpened pencils.

He had plainly been trying.

"It might go easier," I suggested, "if you relaxed for a little while, just forgot about it." I bit back the rest of what I had been about to say. That when I was painting and found I couldn't go on, just stopping and not thinking about it often helped me. But Dwayne wouldn't expect that kind of comment from Fabriana.

His blue eyes moved from the horizon, settled on me briefly.

For a moment, I thought that I had spoken aloud and given myself away. He was staring at me with an open question in his eyes. Then he shifted his gaze away.

"You mustn't worry about last night," I said.

"If I knew what to do, I would do it," he muttered.

"Are you sure there isn't some way I can

help you, Dwayne?"

"I'm afraid not. I'm stuck and that's all there is to it. Both you and Mark will just have to wait until I get myself unraveled." He smiled suddenly, "And it's just as well. After last night I think you're entitled to a day off, don't you?"

"But it's not necessary," I told him. "I'm perfectly all right."

He shuddered. "It was so close, Fabriana. I dreamed about it all night. What it could have been like. And then Charlotte had to make that scene."

"It doesn't matter."

"But it does. She simply keeps all of us stirred up. And it's for nothing. It started on the dig, and she won't let go. I don't know what ails the woman. And poor Rosa, she keeps staring over her shoulder for Mayeroni's ghost. And Karen's so on edge. I keep thinking that she and Hank . . . " Dwayne sighed. "But there I go, spilling over on you again. Go out to the pool. Get some sun on your leg, and spend a few pleasant hours daydreaming. Then maybe you'll forget all about what happened."

"I already have," I told him. But I rose, went to the door. "Come out later, if you feel you can. It might do you some good."

"Perhaps I will," he said.

I went back to my room, changed to Fabriana's bright bikini. It was still substantially more daring than one I would have chosen for myself, but now I found it pretty and comfortable once I had it on.

I freshened my makeup, reminding myself that I must learn to use more eye liner, more shadow. I grinned as I put on the bright lipstick that Fabriana preferred.

Thus far the impersonation had been successful.

Perhaps too successful.

But to maintain it was essential if I were ever to learn the truth about Skeleton Key.

Karen and Hank were at the pool.

She had changed to her lavender bikini. He now wore red briefs. They sat side by side, unmoving, unspeaking. Two very still silhouettes against the brilliance of the sun.

I hesitated, then joined them.

Karen glanced up, her eyes inscrutable behind big dark glasses. "No work today, I gather."

"Your father's not able to go ahead. He said he might come out later," I answered. "Maybe if he relaxes a bit . . . "

"He relaxes entirely too much," Karen snapped. "That's why this whole thing is taking so long. He should have finished the book three months ago, and you know it."

"I'm not writing it, Karen," I answered sharply.

"Of course not. That's not what I mean. But my father is . . . well, let's say he's somehow easily distracted."

"I wouldn't think so," I said coolly. But I wondered what Karen was driving at. Did she believe it was Fabriana's fault that Dwayne hadn't finished his book? Why would she think that? What reason would Fabriana have for wanting to delay Dwayne's work?

Some of these questions were answered almost immediately when Karen said, "And I don't blame you for wanting to distract him, Fabriana. After all, when the book is finished, he won't need this big staff he has now. He'll settle down to plan the next dig, and then we'll be off on it. That's what I'm looking forward to."

Hank said, "Karen, aren't you going too far?"

"I don't see anything wrong in saying what I think." Karen laughed softly. "We three know my father is vulnerable." Her blue eyes swept me. "And why not? What's more natural than that a man should be vulnerable to a pretty girl's charms?"

"What indeed?" I murmured.

"Of course," Karen went on thoughtfully, "a pretty girl might wonder at how easily he transfers his affections." The dark glasses pointed at me suddenly. "First Alice Kane. Then you. Tell me, Fabriana, would you have tried to get him? I mean if she hadn't died?"

"Karen, for God's sake," Hank groaned. "What are you trying to do? If your father heard you he'd brain you." Hank stopped suddenly.

I realized that he was thinking of Alice Kane. His choice of language had been particularly unfortunate.

Karen didn't seem to notice. She arched her brows at him. "What's the big defense deal? Fabriana can take care of herself, as you know."

He chuckled, didn't answer.

"You make me wonder, Hank." She smiled suddenly. "Okay, just tell me. Where were you, Hank, when Fabriana spent her time in Key West? I know you weren't on Skeleton Key all the time."

He laughed louder. "You don't know what you want, so you're grabbing out for trouble with both hands. One day it's me, and one day it's not. I'm a patient man, so I don't mind hanging around and waiting, and I don't even mind if you pretend you're jealous every once in a while, just don't push it too far. Because I might start minding. Just remember that even a patient man can reach the end of the line."

"Hank Darrow, are you threatening me?"

"Just passing you a small amount of information." He got to his feet, tall, golden, his bronze skin aglow with health and virility. He posed for a moment, stretched, and then launched himself in a low flat dive that barely skimmed the surface of the pool. He came up, laughing again, and lifted a lean hand. "Come on, Karen. It won't hurt you to cool off."

She said softly, with an impenetrable sideways look at me, "Maybe he's right. Maybe it won't," and followed him into the water.

Soon after, the two of them came out. They wrapped each other in heavy towels, and went off in search of iced drinks.

I was glad to be alone. I stretched my bruised leg cautiously and turned my face to the sun.

I thought that it was lucky that neither I, nor Fabriana, tanned heavily or burned. Our skins were fair, but somehow impervious. It was only one more thing that could have made the impersonation go all wrong.

For a moment, I wished it had.

I wished that Mark had seen through the mask of makeup the first time he looked at me.

I wished that Dwayne had met me with, "Just a minute. What's going on? You're not Fabriana Harden. So who are you?"

It would have been simpler, easier, if I had been forced to explain, to describe the substitution, simpler then because I could have demanded to know what, or who, Fabriana had sought to escape.

But that was only for a moment. I knew it would never do to be found out. I had to discover the secret of Skeleton Key on my own.

I decided, after a few minutes, to walk down to the marina, then just wander around a bit. The sooner I felt completely at home in my surroundings the safer my secret would be.

I got to my feet, and crossed the patio to the low gate. In the small patio again, I had to pass before Mayeroni. Now he stood in bright sunlight. But it scarcely seemed to touch him. It brought no cheer to his malevolent face. It brought no gentleness to his sightless eyes. I found myself tiptoeing by, and glad to step outside, onto the grassy slope that led down to the dock where the launch drifted next to several canoes I hadn't noticed the day before.

Mark was scrubbing the white hull with a brush. He grinned at me. "Want to help?"

"I'll observe," I told him.

"Then come aboard."

I climbed over the rail, then edged down to the deck. "You look as if you're enjoying yourself, Mark."

More than that, he looked like a small boy allowed to handle a forbidden toy.

"I am enjoying myself, Fab. But I guess I can't stall out here much longer. I'll have to get back to the desk pretty soon." He slanted a glance at me. "As a matter of fact, I was sort of waiting for you."

"For me?"

"I thought, if you decided to go out, you might need some help." He stopped. Then, "No. That's not the truth. I just wanted to suggest that you not go out today."

I didn't know what he meant. I didn't know how to answer him. "Go out?" I thought. I didn't risk a mistake. I asked instead, "If Dwayne's not working, then what's your hurry?"

Mark gave me a quick, puzzled look. "I have to keep going with the polishing, you know. The more of that I can do as we go along, the faster the end of the book will come."

"Oh, of course," I said hastily. "I thought you were up to date on that."

He worked over the hull, whistling between his teeth. Then he straightened up, and put the brush and rags aside. "I guess that's it."

"Very nice," I observed, regretful that I had spent so much time at the pool with Hank and Karen when I might have been down here with Mark.

"Not that I'm really in a hurry to go in," he observed. "I just think the sooner we finish the job the better."

"Karen agrees with you," I told him.

He raised his dark brows over narrowing eyes.

"She was just telling me, not quite directly, but almost, that if I distracted Dwayne less, he might work more."

"Was she?" Mark grinned. "I imagine that you answered her properly."

"I didn't quite know what to say," I told him, and then added quickly, "and I didn't see any use in arguing with her about it anyway."

"It's true enough that you distract Dwayne, Fab."

"Mark!" I protested.

He laughed softly. "You distract most men, don't you? And don't give me that shocked rejecting look. You know perfectly well that you're aware of your attractiveness and make use of it when you have to."

I didn't try to answer him. Fabriana certainly was aware of her charms, and had always used them to advantage. I, with my own point of view about life, had always tended to think in other terms.

But I confessed to myself then that I did

find it enjoyable to have Mark looking at me with such warm approval.

I wondered suddenly how Fabriana had felt about him. I would have expected her to choose him over Dwayne. Yet Dwayne was most certainly in love with her. And she must have given him reason to hope. Perhaps she had a motive about which I knew nothing.

Mark was frowning at me, his approval suddenly gone. He swung away, saying gruffly, "I'm going up to the house now. Do you want me to get your canoe out first?"

I nodded, not quite sure of what he was talking about, but certain from his tone, from what he had said before, that this was a service he had often performed for Fabriana.

"Not that I think you ought to go out today, Fab. I don't. If I thought I could talk you out of it, I would," he went on.

"I don't like to break old habits," I said lightly. "I'll go."

He swung off the launch, jerked a canoe into the dock.

I followed, allowed him to help me in.

He thrust the paddle at me. "Okay. If you're sure you mean it."

"Why not?" I grinned.

He shrugged. With a quick nod, he turned, went quickly up the shell-lined path to the house.

I rested on the paddle, feeling the slow drift of the canoe. I was not afraid of the boat, nor of the sea. Fabriana and I had both learned to take care of ourselves, though she had never learned to swim as well as I.

The buoys suddenly bobbed and shifted, their warning gongs floating on the still sultry air.

When Mark turned to look back at me, I set the paddle in and stroked hard.

It was pleasant to feel the full expansion of my strength as I flexed my arm, putting shoulder and waist into movement. The canoe lurched, then moved smoothly away from the marina.

The short dark shadows of the palms slid along the white beach as I drifted by. Teeth of coral rock glimmered just beneath the surface of the sea. I decided not to risk the channel. I wasn't familiar enough with it. I set out for the end of the island, staying close in, intending to circle it.

Soon, tired, I rested, allowing the current to take me. The canoe moved on to the tip of Skeleton Key, the house was lost in the fringed palms. I steered carefully past a shallow spot, and was suddenly in shadow. The character of the shoreline had completely changed. Huge banyan trees arched overhead, thick coiling roots seemed to strike deep into greasy-looking swamplands. The sea was stronger here, darker, the currents pulled and sucked around me.

I put more strength into my strokes, and found that it took almost all my effort to control the boat.

Had Fabriana made a practice of canoeing around the island? I wondered.

It seemed unlike her to expend all that much effort for a few hours exercise. Even the pleasure of being alone, off and away from the others, could hardly have led her to struggle through these dangerous tides.

Suddenly, as I thought that, I realized that I felt water on my bare feet.

It was cool, salty. I wondered where it had come from. I hadn't splashed when I stroked.

The canoe moved sluggishly now along the shore but a good way out. The banyans and palms and pines seemed to form a jungle. I hadn't expected anything like that on Skeleton Key.

It was green, shadowy, strangely still.

The house seemed so far away now.

There was nothing but the sea, nothing but the reaching shade of the huge trees.

Now there was water at my ankles.

I stared at it. I stared at the growing pool on the bottom of the canoe.

I had nothing to bail with.

With that thought, I realized that bailing wouldn't help.

What had been a trickle became a flood.

I saw the gaping hole just below the water line. I saw the flap that covered it suddenly break free and float away.

The canoe lurched.

The sea gurgled around me, and rose up, and rose more. And suddenly the seat under me had settled and fallen away.

I felt myself sinking and sinking.

I knew I must save myself or drown.

Chapter 8

In those first moments of panic, I fought for air, for freedom from the blind darkness that seemed to enfold me.

I kicked and struggled, with brilliant sparks bursting behind my squinting eyes, and sky-rocketing pains exploding in my lungs and throat.

Finally I broke through to the surface.

Warm air touched my wet cheeks. Hard sun stung my eyes.

I gasped and sank in sudden weakness. I was further from the shore than I had thought. The canoe, still afloat, but overturned, was drifting farther out each moment. The paddle, moving with the current, was way beyond my reach already.

I went down, swallowing brackish water. But that time I didn't struggle. I held my breath, kicked hard, and rose to the surface with limbs and mind under control.

Once again my eyes searched for the canoe. A single glance confirmed what I had seen dimly before. I couldn't hope to reach it, to cling to it for safety. I took a deep breath, and looked landward where my only chance lay.

The coral island glowed white with a rim of jungle green at the water line. It seemed much farther away now than when I had come around the point. It seemed, somehow, much farther than I could manage to swim.

But I had no choice.

I launched myself into slow and careful movement. I stroked easily, trying not to expend my strength too quickly.

But it took tremendous effort to make headway against the outgoing tide, and with each kick, my bruised leg seemed to tighten more, hurt more.

I stroked, and counted, and stroked again.

I kept my eyes fixed on the shadow of the banyan trees.

When my breath was gone, and it was much too quickly, I allowed myself to float, but only briefly. For at the instant of rest, I learned that the tide took me, and I lost ground so that the island seemed to recede into a red haze.

I struggled on, so intent on reaching shore that there was no room in my mind then for question or speculation. No room for the remembering of a torn flap below the water line, a flap that peeled away in a four-inch patch, and floated out of sight. There was, I recall now, no room in my mind even for fear.

My essence, soul, body and will contracted into a single drive. But the bright island seemed more and more distant, the rim of green shadow paler and smaller.

Gradually I found that my body became more and more resistant to my concentrated will. The sea around me seemed gentle and kind. I felt that I could sink in it and rest. I felt that I could sleep softly and safely in its arms.

The beat of blood in my head, the racing of my pulses, the gasp of breath in my throat became a roar of sound that enveloped me in a net of desperation, and forced my weakening senses into a temporary retreat.

I was so near unconsciousness when I felt myself gripped, caught and held, that I mistook my rescuer for the sea itself. I fought it in a last waning surge of strength, and then, with my face close to Mark's, seeing him through a rainbow of tears and sea, I cried, "I can't make it, Mark. It's just too far to go," and I felt myself go limp in his arms.

It was a strange few moments. Strengthless myself, I was aware of his strength. Too tired to move, I knew that he was swimming with me.

We were suddenly on firm ground, floundering in the banyan roots, sinking in bottomless swamp.

He half-carried, half-dragged me through them, and we left the swampy rim behind. He laid me gently to rest on the shore.

"Rest, Fab. I'll go and get some help."

I caught his hand. "No, wait. Don't leave me, Mark."

"It's over," he said. "You're safe. Stay here. I'll get Dwayne and Hank." He got to his feet.

I pushed myself up, swaying, breathless. I stood beside him.

He was staring out to sea. "I want that canoe," he muttered.

"It's gone, Mark."

He turned his head slowly, narrow eyes scanning the view before us. He asked, without looking at me, "What happened?"

With returned strength, there came returning thought. I felt the canoe sink beneath me. I saw the patch rip away. I knew that I had been meant to drown.

His face had suddenly developed new lines. He was very still. "Fab, you've never had trouble handling that canoe before. You've been out in it every day since I came to Skeleton Key. I want to know what happened today."

"I think there was a patch below the water line. I think it opened up."

"Just like that?"

I nodded.

"Are you sure you didn't scrape a reef? Go aground when you turned the point?"

"No. It's impossible. I saw how shallow it was there. I was very careful."

"Another weird accident," he said softly.

But now I was remembering that he had been working on the launch. He had been alone. I remembered that he had suggested that I take the canoe out, offered to help me with it. I hated the suspicion that flooded through me. I quickly reminded myself that Mark had just saved my life. Why, if he had meant me to die, would he have saved me?

Then how was it that he had said he was going into the house to work, and instead he had crossed the island, presumably on foot, and been on the shore to save me?

I brushed my soaked and tousled hair from my eyes. I was suddenly unbearably afraid. Afraid of my own thoughts.

For this was no weird accident. No more than the fall of the wardrobe the night before had been a weird accident.

Someone was determined that I, that Fabriana, be killed. So determined as to have made two attempts in two days.

Twice death had struck at me. And twice I had just managed to escape its grasping fingers.

Mark was looking at me, his pale eyes narrowed in what was becoming a familiar bewilderment. "I didn't realize that you can swim as well as you do, Fab. I knew you could manage. But just now, before you were exhausted, you were doing so well that for a minute I couldn't believe it was you."

"It was me," I said briefly. Then, "It's lucky for me that you were here. I thought you were going to work."

"I was." He paused. Then, "But I decided to have a walk first. To clear my head."

"I see."

But I didn't see. I wondered if his being on this side of Skeleton Key had really been just a coincidence. I wondered if he knew I would founder, if he had been checking up on me, watching to see if I drowned, my body floated away on the tide, never to be seen again. Was he Fabriana's enemy?

He had told me earlier that Fabriana always canoed around the island, and I had told him that I wouldn't want to break an old habit. But why would Fabriana do that regularly?

Mark was saying, "When I realized that it *was* you, I couldn't figure out what had happened. After all, you know this shoreline so well. You've been coming past here every day for weeks and weeks, haven't you?"

Then Fabriana must have done just that. Perhaps that was why Mark, or someone else, had known I would do it again today. Perhaps that was why it was assumed that I would sink with the sinking canoe and drown.

Mark was waiting, his eyes full of something I couldn't read. It might have been suspicion. It might have been a dawning certainty.

I said, "I've always liked the exercise, Mark." And then, lightly, "You haven't been spying on me, have you?"

He didn't answer that. Instead he said, "Promise me that you won't come here any more. At least not alone."

I didn't have time to answer him.

There was a sudden whisper of sound from the brush, and the green shadows danced on the shore.

Hank appeared from within them, and stood there, looking first at me, and then at Mark.

"I hope I'm not interrupting an assignation," he grinned finally.

Neither Mark nor I answered him.

He swept us both with his green eyes. "What's going on? That's supposed to be a joke. Laugh for me, won't you? Now I see you're both soaked. I can understand it in you, Fab. You're in your bikini and you took a swim. Okay. But what about you, Mark? Have you taken to swimming in the sea fully clothed?"

Mark took a long slow breath before he replied, "Fab had another accident. The canoe split or something. I happened by and saw her thrashing around so I went in and got her out."

Hank whistled softly, "Another accident, you say?"

"It looks like one anyhow," Mark retorted.

First Mark, I thought.

Now Hank.

I shivered.

Had Mark crossed the island to watch from the shore while I went down for the last time? If so, why had he bothered to save me?

Or had Hank come to observe my death? And been foiled by Mark.

Hank's green eyes searched my face carefully. "You know what," he said after a moment, "I'm beginning to think I don't believe in so many accidents."

"If you start Charlotte's song and dance now . . ." Mark stopped, took another deep breath.

"No," Hank grinned. "I'm not even going to mention Mayeroni." He looked me up and down. "But you, Fab. I'm beginning to wonder if maybe you've got some deep buried need to be the center of attention. I wonder if you're contriving all this."

"That's not worth answering," I gasped.

He shrugged his broad bronze shoulders, grinned again. "Okay. How about this? Suppose you have some deep need to destroy yourself?"

"That's not worth answering either," Mark snapped.

"Then I've just run out of suggestions," Hank told him.

Mark didn't answer. He turned to me. "Can you make it back now?"

I nodded.

He tucked a hand under my arm, led the way, with Hank following, into the green shadows.

Stumbling, still exhausted, my leg really aching now, I allowed myself to be drawn along.

It was clear to me now that Fabriana had not been exaggerating when she first said her life was in danger. I'd known it the night before, again this morning when I examined the wardrobe legs. I hadn't needed further proof, but it had been offered to me. Fabriana was surrounded by the threat of death. She had sent me to Skeleton Key to take her place. She was willing to let me die.

I dare not waste time being hurt, cozening unspoken reproaches. What was important now was to identify her enemy, the enemy now mine.

Why did that unknown someone want to see Fabriana dead?

What had she done?

What did she know?

To whom was she a threat?

My own life, as well as hers, depended on my ability to search out the truth and find it.

"I still can't get over the way you managed to swim, Fab," Mark was saying thoughtfully.

Hank put in, "Name it desperation. When someone knows he has only that chance he learns pretty fast."

"I guess so," Mark answered, but he somehow didn't sound convinced.

I was sure that he was wondering if Fabriana had only pretended before to be a fairly poor swimmer, and if so, why she had.

The house loomed up ahead, set like a silvered jewel in its manicured lawns. I noticed suddenly that the manicure of the lawns was not quite as good as I would have expected, and remembered then that the gardener, Mickey Hendle, had died two months before.

I was startled that it had taken so little time to cross the island. But I didn't mention that. I was only thankful for it. Fabriana, of course, would have been expected to know that Skeleton Key was very long but quite narrow.

Hank suddenly ducked ahead of Mark and

me. "I'm going to alert the others, tell Rosa to get some tea ready."

"Wait," Mark said.

Hank paused. "What for?"

"Maybe it's no use getting everybody upset."

Hank went on, calling over his shoulder. "They might as well know about it. One look at Fabriana's face and they'll realize something's happened."

When we were quite alone, Mark stopped me. We were at the side gate then. I knew that just beyond, in the small patio, Mayeroni would be waiting. A shiver went over me.

Mark tipped my chin up, peered into my eyes. "Fab, you've been here about a year now, haven't you?"

I nodded.

"Isn't that long enough for you?"

"I don't know what you mean," I quavered.

But of course I did know. And I knew what was coming, too.

"Don't you think that it might be time for you to push on?"

I stiffened. "Why should I, Mark?"

He didn't answer that. He said, "There must be a lot of jobs you can get. In a lot of interesting places."

"But this is a good job, Mark."

"Is that why you stay on? Or do you have another reason?"

"Another reason?" I echoed.

"Is it because of Dwayne?"

My cheeks burned. I felt the blush rise up and betray me, and then suddenly drain away. I said sharply, "That's none of your business."

"That's just what you've told me before," he said sadly, "but I somehow feel that it *is* my business. Especially now."

"Why now?" I stopped, then went on in a whisper, "Do you mean because you've saved my life?"

"Maybe that's what I mean," he said. "But maybe it isn't."

I didn't ask him to explain that. I turned from him, stepped through the gate, leaving the green shadows of the jungle behind. The patio sun was hard and bright and blinding, but there was goose flesh on my arms and legs.

Mayeroni's sightless eyes glared at me through the palmettos.

Mark stopped me once more. "So much has happened, Fab. Alice. And Mickey. And in these last two days, you yourself have had two really narrow escapes. Not to mention what happened before then. Don't you see that it goes on and on? Don't you understand what a risk you're taking?"

I raised my eyes to his, demanded, "Why

do you want me to leave Skeleton Key? Why are you trying to drive me away?"

His lips tightened. His pale eyes seemed suddenly shuttered. He turned away without answering me.

At that moment, Charlotte burst from the house, crying shrilly, "Fabriana, what happened? Hank said that you nearly drowned. Mark, is she all right? Where's Dwayne? Does he know?"

"Charlotte, please . . . " I protested. "You can see that I'm perfectly okay. Don't . . . "

"You went canoeing the way you do every day, didn't you?" she went on. "But nothing happened before this. The boats are fine. They are. I know they are. They've always been fine. So what could have gone wrong? Tell me, Fabriana."

She didn't give me time to say anything. She seized me by the arm, pulled me with her along the path to my room. She chattered and fussed while she pulled dry clothes from the closet, and helped me undress and wrapped me in a white towel.

I finally gathered myself for resistance when she began to push me toward the bed.

"Get in. You have to keep warm. Rosa will be here with tea right away. You have to take off the chill. I just don't understand any of it."

But it was Charlotte's teeth that were chattering, her hands that shook.

I was calm now.

Charlotte was in a state close to hysteria again.

I protested that I didn't need such attentions. I was recovered from my dunking and from my swim.

"Oh, but you're so lucky," Charlotte cried. "Suppose you'd gotten tired, or had a cramp? Suppose you'd gone down in that tide? And do you know, your body might never have been found. We'd never have known . . ."

I shivered then. I preferred not to think so graphically about what might have happened. I said gently, "But it wasn't like that, Charlotte. So there's nothing to worry about, is there?"

Her nervous chatter came to a sudden stop. Her blue eyes looked dull, her skin a sallow net of tightening wrinkles. "But it could still happen," she faltered. "Don't you realize? Every minute that you're on Skeleton Key you're in terrible danger."

"But why?" I asked breathlessly. "What have I done?"

I thought that here, at last, I was to learn what I needed to know.

"It's the treasure," Charlotte whispered. "God help us all. It has to be the treasure, and

Mayeroni's curse. Dwayne and his greed will bring us all to our ends."

I drew a deep disappointed breath. I said, "Dwayne says there is no treasure, there might never have been."

Charlotte's lips twisted sourly. "That's what he *says*."

"But you were with him on the dig, Charlotte. Surely, if there had been jewels, ornaments, you'd know where they were, how he hid them."

"I don't know that, and thank you, I don't want to," Charlotte retorted. "But I don't believe that he didn't find it. He must have."

"But why do you say that?" I demanded. "If you have no proof there was a treasure, then why do you think . . . "

"Mayeroni," Charlotte insisted. "Alice Kane. Mickey Hendle. They're both dead, aren't they? It must be Mayeroni's curse that killed them. And it would have killed them only if the treasure were threatened." She paused. Then she went on in a harsh whisper. "It has to be that, don't you see? What else could explain what's happening here?"

I sighed. Charlotte's reasoning seemed too weak to be taken seriously. Yet surely she was convinced that she was right. Or was she? Was she pretending?

I couldn't tell.

For all I knew Charlotte might possess information that she wouldn't pass on to me. Perhaps she was too frightened to offer more definite proof. But even if she were right, and there had been a treasure, could I believe in the Mayeroni legend? Could I accept his curse?

Rosa came waddling in, clucking and asking questions.

Charlotte imperiously cut her off, took the tray from her, and sent her away, though poor Rosa obviously wanted to linger.

Then, thrusting a cup of steaming tea into my hands, Charlotte said in a sharp whisper, "I think if you had any sense, Fabriana, you'd know what to do. You'd run away from Skeleton Key. You'd forget Dwayne, and the job, and the treasure, too. You'd just take yourself away from here for good."

Chapter 9

Take yourself away from here for good.

Long after Charlotte left me alone to rest, the words echoed through my mind.

The room seemed to close in on me, the walls whispering, the orange glow of the closed drapes seemed to dissolve into flame.

I knew now what Fabriana must have felt building up in her those days before she finally wrote her plea for help.

I understood now that terror that Fabriana had lived with. It was my own terror now.

I could leave, of course, and leave the terror far behind.

But what of Fabriana?

Why had she been unwilling to leave?

Why had she felt that I must take her place, play her part, be her instead of myself, for two weeks?

Had she willingly offered me to the reaching threat? Or had she, as so often when we were children, simply drawn me in, without thinking what that could mean?

It was something that had begun so long before. Begun almost as a joke. I had been the elder by ten minutes. "You must take care of your baby sister," our parents had always said. I had tried to until I began to feel the gradual sapping of my own identity. Then, resisting, I had tried to draw back from Fabriana, to change my way of dress, my hair style. When I saw her reaction I knew that I could save myself only by being away from her. It hadn't been easy to take that step, but I had managed it. I had managed it in spite of her rage and my regret. And there was regret. We were sisters, twins; we had always been together. I loved her. But I had known my survival depended on my ability to maintain my own identity. I believed that Fabriana's survival depended on the same thing. But she had called out to me, and I had come . . .

At last exhaustion claimed me. I slept and dreamed of nights in a distant jungle, and leaping flames flickering on golden ornaments and huge uncut jewels that glowed with living light. I dreamed of shrinking maidens at the edge of a bottomless pit. I dreamed of azure seas suddenly black, rising to engulf me.

I awakened suddenly, my heart beating too quickly. My senses were immediately alert to a new threat. I realized that I would be in that state as long as I stayed on Skeleton Key.

Dwayne stood in the doorway. "I'm sorry. I

frightened you, didn't I? I didn't mean to." He came in, sank heavily into the chair beside the bed. "Mark's been telling me what happened. Or at least what he thinks happened."

I said, "I'm afraid it was a near miss, Dwayne. If he hadn't been there to help me I'd never have made it to shore."

"I always worried about you canoeing all the way out there by yourself. Somehow, I had the feeling that if anything went wrong . . . "

"But I managed," I cut in, "with Mark's help, of course. And then Hank came along, too."

"You're sure you're not the worse for wear?"

"Oh, no. I'll get up in a minute. I've had a nap. There's no need for me to stay in bed."

"You've been through too much in the last few days, Fabriana."

I allowed the silence to hang between us. Then, smiling faintly, I said, "Charlotte insists it was Mayeroni's work again."

"She will let her imagination run away with her. I oughtn't to have taken her on the expedition with me. And if I'd known what would happen I certainly wouldn't have."

"But, Dwayne, if there really was a treasure . . . "

He stared at me, his blue eyes blank,

shuttered, unreadable.

The room seemed to darken. The orange glow seemed to deepen.

He said finally, "That's a myth, Fabriana. I've told you often enough. And it's written about in the book."

I nodded thoughtfully.

"No one will ever find the treasure. No one will ever desecrate Mayeroni's holy place," Dwayne went on.

"If there is a treasure to find, you mean," I put in softly.

"If . . . and there isn't."

"But somehow everyone does believe in it," I answered. "You know they do, Dwayne. Charlotte, and Karen, too. And Hank, I imagine."

"It's what they want to believe."

"Once they accept the idea of the treasure, they seem to accept the idea of Mayeroni's curse," I pointed out.

"Foolish minds. They should know better. We do, don't we, Fabriana?"

But I did not know the truth. Yet I couldn't admit to my ignorance. I had begun to see too many questions in Dwayne's eyes now.

Somehow I had managed to say something to him that troubled him.

I stretched, sat up. "I think I'll dress now, Dwayne."

He stared at me, then rose. "Yes. We might as well pretend that nothing has happened one more time."

Bitterness burned in his voice, clouded his eyes. He stood over me. "Fabriana, don't let this change things. Remember that our problem isn't Mayeroni, will you?"

No matter what Dwayne told me, I decided, the problems of Skeleton Key seemed to go back to the Mayeroni myth, to the original archaeological expedition which had drawn everyone together. To the treasure which Dwayne denied, and everyone else believed in.

The next two weeks proved a strange anticlimax to the terror of my first two days on the island.

I waited, cautiously aware that soon there must be another attack on me. But nothing happened.

Dwayne couldn't settle down to work, but I attended to his correspondence for him, did a variety of errands, but tried to avoid being alone with him as much as I could.

I sensed the growing tension in him, and it frightened me even more. Plainly he would soon no longer contain the feelings he had for Fabriana. He would declare himself. And then I would be forced to tell him the truth. I would never allow him to expose his heart to me, believing that I was someone else.

I waited for some clue, some sign, of who was Fabriana's enemy, who intended that Fabriana should die. But instead of gaining insight, I became more and more confused.

Mark had told me to leave Skeleton Key because I was in danger. I wondered if concern for me was the real reason. Or if he had another motive. He asked so many questions. He seemed to turn up so opportunely.

Charlotte had warned me to go away for good, warning me of Mayeroni's curse. Did she really believe that the dead priest could harm me? Or was she more and more aware of Dwayne's concentration on me? Was she jealous of her position in the household?

Karen vacillated between friendliness and malice, but I had observed that she responded with the same inconsistency to Hank. She seemed to view us both with a certain suspicion. As if she thought that Hank and I had a bond in common.

If there had been such a bond between Fabriana and Hank, I knew nothing of it. He treated me with a certain gentle amusement that I found relaxing. Yet I wondered if it concealed a carefully buried animosity.

I found myself making the full circle in my suspicions. I began to think that it might be

Dwayne himself that Fabriana feared. Yet if there were a reason for it, he had never revealed it to me.

I had thought myself fairly well prepared when Fabriana briefed me for my stay in Skeleton Key. Now I knew that she had sent me here as if blinded and lame. I wondered if she had expected me to be successful in the impersonation she planned.

I waited, edgy by day and sleepless by night, for the fingers of death to stretch from the shadows to clench around me. Nothing happened.

I waited for two weeks to pass, remembering my other life, my real life, distantly. As if the shuttered cottage were a dream, Mr. Pierce's whistle a fantasy, my painting and Ryson and Davis no more than wishful thinking.

Soon after Mark had rescued me from the sea, I crossed the island on foot. I hoped that the canoe had been washed ashore and that I could find it. I wanted to see if I could find solid proof, as I had with the wardrobe, that the boat had been deliberately damaged.

Mark had found me searching among the banyan roots.

I didn't know how long he had been silently watching me, nor what to answer, when he suddenly stepped out of the shadows, demanded, "What do you think you're doing here, Fab?"

I gasped. "Mark, have you been following me?"

"No. But maybe I should be."

"I think I can manage quite well alone," I retorted.

"Do you?"

I remembered his arms around me, towing me, holding me, fighting the current to bring me to shore. I felt heat burn in my cheeks. I whispered, "I'm sorry, Mark. I'm afraid that you frightened me so when you came out of the trees that I lost the good sense I ought to have."

He eyed me, plainly bewildered. "You oughtn't to wander around alone, Fab."

"Then you know," I said. "You're certain, aren't you?"

He raised his dark brows, obviously refusing to commit himself until I put my meaning into words.

I said softly, "There have been two attempts on my life, haven't there? Perhaps even more."

"I think so," he answered.

"But why? What have I done? Why would anyone want to kill me?"

"I think you'd know that better than anyone else," he told me.

156

"But I don't know."

"I wish I could believe you, Fab. I want to, yet I can't."

"I have no reason to lie," I told him.

But I wondered. How did I know what Fabriana had done? How did I know what had happened here on Skeleton Key before I came to take her place?

Mark demanded, "What about Alice Kane? Would you lie about her?"

"Mark! What do you mean?"

"It was such a still night," he said softly. "Rosa told me all about it. A still night. No breeze. Not a breath of air. A silence that was fit for a graveyard. Yet a coconut fell. It fell from a date palm, a tree on which there are no coconuts! It killed Alice Kane!"

I stared at him. "You think she was murdered."

"There's something odd about her death," he said firmly.

"But I . . . why would I . . . "

"She was so beautiful. That piled-high red hair. Those shining green eyes. That tall, lithe body." He took a deep breath. "Rosa told me," he repeated. "And then you came, Fab."

I was speechless. I shivered at the possibility he had presented to me.

Was this then what Fabriana had feared so?

The accusation that she had murdered Alice Kane?

"She had a right to live," Mark was saying. "She had a right to love Dwayne Fuller."

Something in Mark's voice, his words, told me the truth. Mark had known Alice Kane more intimately than he had admitted to me. Mark had loved Alice.

I finally managed to say, "I had nothing to do with Alice Kane's death, Mark. You must believe me."

He didn't reply. His narrowed eyes searched my face for a long time. Finally he said, "Of course it could have been an accident, couldn't it? And Mickey Hendle could have died by accident, too. Even an agile eighteen-year-old can fall from the rock where he's been fishing and hit his head and drown."

Now I knew a lot more than I had before about the two deaths that had occurred before I came to Skeleton Key. But what I knew only gave me greater cause for bewilderment.

I began to see why Charlotte laid the trouble on Mayeroni's curse. That made as much sense as no explanation at all.

Mark said then, "If I weren't afraid that there's more to come, I wouldn't be so worried."

I very nearly told him the truth then. I

wanted to. I wanted to explain, share my fear. I wanted to trust him.

Yet how could I?

How could I be sure he was not himself involved?

He had suggested removing the wardrobe immediately after it had fallen. I didn't know if he had examined it later, or wanted to keep me from examining it.

He had suggested I take out the canoe, and helped me into it. I didn't know if he had assumed I would want to, because Fabriana always had. Or because he had prepared it to entrap me.

Now he said very quietly, "If you were looking for what remained of the canoe, I might as well tell you that I searched the whole shore two hours ago. I found a part of the canoe."

"What did you do with it?"

"I put it in a safe place."

"But where?"

"I don't think that's something you need to know."

"I don't?" I cried. "It's my life that is threatened."

"You know how to save it, Fabriana," he answered, and turned and left me alone.

I shivered, knowing what he meant. I could go away, leave Skeleton Key for good, leave the danger behind me, seek safety and find it, forgetting the accursed island forever.

Mark didn't know that I couldn't leave. Not now. Not until I could see Fabriana, talk to her.

I didn't know what would happen if I were to expose the deception we had joined in together. I didn't know what it might do to her.

The next afternoon, remembering what Mark had told me about Alice Kane, the veiled accusation he had made, I tried to speak to Rosa about Alice.

She shrugged her plump shoulders. She said, embarrassed and a little afraid, "Too many women in one house. That's what happens. You can't have too many women for a man. It makes trouble." She veiled her dark eyes. "It's up to him, the man. He has to control it. If he won't, then the women try to."

I realized that she was trying to say that she didn't blame me, didn't blame Fabriana, for what had happened. I supposed she was remembering her conversation with Mark, and regretting it.

There was nothing more I could ask her. I changed the subject.

But I didn't forget my initial impression that Mark had loved Alice Kane. It sank deep into my consciousness, spreading continuous ripples like a pebble in a pond. I carried that awareness with me always, not understanding why it troubled me so.

One more incident worth remarking on occurred during that time. Karen and Hank had gone into Key West, having invited me to go with them. I had decided to stay on Skeleton Key.

Later, when they returned, Karen stormed into the living room, her eyes aglow with triumph, to cry, "Fabriana, how did you manage to sneak off the island?"

I had been playing cards with Dwayne. I lowered my hand, gave her an astonished glance. "What?"

"I saw you, you know. You can't pretend that you weren't in Casey's bar."

"You saw me?" I repeated steadily.

Fabriana . . .

She had been there.

She was in Casey's bar, carelessly allowing herself to be seen.

She had said she wanted to spend two weeks away from the island with a man.

But she was in Key West.

"Of course it was you. You slipped out the second I saw you, but I know I didn't make a mistake."

Hank chuckled. "Karen, what did I tell you? Here's Fabriana. And I'll bet she's been here all evening long."

"I have," I answered. I glanced at Dwayne.

Dwayne nodded, "You must be seeing things, Karen. Fabriana's been in this room, with me."

Mark, sprawled on the sofa, was watching.

I saw the frown gather on his forehead. I saw his eyes narrow and his mouth tighten.

Karen said, "Are you sure? Really?"

Dwayne nodded.

Hank said disgustedly, "You'll never listen, will you, Karen? I told you the minute I saw her . . ."

Karen stared at me. "But I could have sworn . . ."

"And falsely," Dwayne told her. His glance caressed me. "Shall we go on with the game?"

I nodded, tried to concentrate. But I was glad when Dwayne finally yawned, said that he had had enough and went to bed.

Soon after I retired to my room.

Fabriana was in Key West. Within four days I would meet her. We would make our exchange. I would insist on that no matter what she said. I would be free of Skeleton Key forever.

But I fell asleep remembering the sound of his voice when Mark spoke Alice's name. I fell asleep remembering my certainty that he loved her.

Those last four days were so uneventful, so

full of peace and stillness, that it was almost as if the threat on Skeleton Key had been a dream, a suspicion conjured up by Fabriana's words. I knew the truth, but I still found myself wondering if she had exaggerated, distorted, or just plain lied, to get me to take her place. It was what I wanted to believe. It was easier than accepting the promise of threatening death.

It was the morning of what I thought would be my final day there. I sat beside the pool, a pad on my knees

Dwayne had said that he wanted to dictate a few letters to me, and would be out in a little while.

As I waited, I idly sketched a head, a pair of shoulders. I didn't realize what I was doing. It was habitual to me to draw the moment I felt a pencil between my fingers. The face took form, the body.

Then a shadow fell across the page.

Karen said, "What's that?" in a shrill voice.

I slid my hand over the drawing, but I wasn't quite quick enough.

Karen bent closer. "I could swear . . . " She tugged my hand away. "Come on, let me see. I could swear that's Hank Darrow himself." She gave a hoot of triumph. "It is!" Her wide grin suddenly died. She turned a hard cold look on me. "I didn't know you could draw like that. You've been here a whole year, and you never said . . . "

I cursed myself for being so careless. I was certain that Fabriana had not sketched at all on Skeleton Key. Fabriana's talent had been small, and never developed. She had come to hate art as my talent became evident.

I swallowed hard, said, "Oh, that's not drawing. I was doodling."

"But it is Hank. There's no doubt about that." Karen's eyes narrowed. "Why are you drawing him?"

I shrugged. "I don't have the faintest idea."

"I'm getting some ideas," Karen said coldly. "As a matter of fact, those ideas are something I've had for some time! You just leave Hank alone. He's mine, Fabriana, and I don't intend to share him with anybody else."

"Who is whose?" Dwayne inquired suddenly, his mahogany face appearing just beyond Karen's bent head.

She snatched the pad, thrust it at him. "Take a look for yourself. See how you like it."

Dwayne smiled tiredly, but his eyes sought mine questioningly. Aloud he answered, "It's quite a good job."

Karen's body stiffened inside her tan pants suit. Her eyes burned at me, then she stalked away angrily.

Plainly she was jealous of me, of any possible interest of mine in Hank. Yet she herself blew hot and cold with him. I had no time to think about that.

Dwayne's tired smile had faded. "You keep coming up with new talents, Fabriana."

"That's not a talent."

I couldn't tell if the sadness in his eyes was because he, like Karen, thought me interested in Hank, or if it meant he had at last realized that I was not Fabriana.

I set myself to deal with whatever came.

But Dwayne shrugged, said, "Shall we get on with it?" and waited for me to poise my pencil over the pad he had given back to me.

When I was ready, he began to dictate in a low steady voice.

It was after dinner. I had waited until then to tell Dwayne that I would like to go into Key West for the evening and then stay over night.

He said, "Of course. If you want to, Fabriana. I'll speak to Mark about taking you in."

"Again?" Charlotte asked. "I begin to think you have a boyfriend you've never told us about."

"It's the girl I've mentioned before," I said quickly. "The one I went in to meet last time. We arranged it then. I suppose I should have told you. It just never occurred to me."

"Oh," Charlotte said thoughtfully. "I see, I see."

The launch cut through the dark of the sea, past the tolling buoys and their swinging light. It touched the marina gently.

Mark looped a hawser over a piling.

"Shall I walk you to the motel?" he asked.

"Oh, no," I said. "That's certainly not necessary."

"It's pretty dark, pretty late, Fab."

"There's nothing to be afraid of," I answered.

"Not here, you mean."

I was stubbornly silent. It was almost over now. I had nothing more to say to him. I turned to climb to the dock.

He helped me up, then handed me the weekend case I had brought with me.

"I'll pick you up tomorrow. What time?"

"Nine or ten or so. About like now, if that's convenient for you."

"Sure," he answered.

I hesitated for just a moment.

I was going to meet Fabriana. When nine o'clock the next night came, I would be on my way north and home, back to my small cottage, to my easel and paints, to the sweet quiet life I had made for myself. No matter what Fabriana said, did, or promised, I would never return to Skeleton Key. I would never see Mark again.

I found it hard to smile, to give him a casual wave, to go away forever without even saying goodbye.

Chapter 10

Enrico stood behind the desk in the Seaside Motel, looking as if he hadn't moved since I last saw him two weeks before.

He grinned, said, "You got your regular cabin. Number 10. That okay with you?"

"That's fine."

"It's pretty late. You're out of luck if you want any dinner, I guess."

"Oh, I've eaten."

He had made the necessary chitchat easy for me. Now I felt free to ask, "Was anybody looking for me?"

"You mean that good-looking blonde friend of yours?"

I nodded.

"Not yet. I wouldn't forget her if I did see her, would I?" He grinned. "Don't worry. I'll send her back to you when she turns up."

I thanked him, said good night, and took the cottage key. I walked under the pink and yellow lit palms, past the tank of tropical fish. The air was sultry, damp. Wind snapped in the fronds of the tall trees.

I tried not to be disappointed.

I had been hoping that Fabriana would already be there, waiting for me. But I realized now that hadn't been a practical expectation.

Fabriana wouldn't have wanted to give Enrico too long or close a look at her.

The cottage was just as I remembered it. I switched on the television set and watched a panel show for a little while.

Then, bored, I found stationery in the bedside table, and sat at the window to sketch the shadows of the trees outside.

It was pleasant to relax, to be alone, to allow myself to be myself. Now with the restraints put aside, I became aware of how much strain there had been in trying to be Fabriana. But it was over. When she came, I knew I would have to be very firm, perhaps even cruel. I would insist that I would not go back to Skeleton Key, and I would insist that Fabriana not go back either. Whatever threat it was that hung over her there, I could neither exorcise, nor control. So there was, reasonably, only the one thing to do.

I must challenge Fabriana on every count.

I must tell her that she had sent me into danger I couldn't handle, that I knew she had risked my life for hers. Once she knew everything that had happened on Skeleton Key, perhaps she would understand what she had done. Perhaps she would agree, and turn her back on the past. The decision, and the responsibility, would have to be hers. I would leave for home immediately either way.

I braced myself for the coming meeting.

But as the hours went by, I became more frightened.

I waited, ears attuned to every sound out of doors. When more hours had passed, I still waited, dozing, but with hope fading.

Fabriana did not come.

Through the long night, through the whole of the following day, I clung to those sagging remnants of hope, still refusing to make plans, to think.

But when evening came again, and the pink and yellow lights outlined the palms in the courtyard, I knew a decision had to be made.

Fabriana had not returned.

I hadn't heard from her.

I was certain that she was somewhere in Key West. Karen had seen her in Casey's bar.

I didn't know what had happened to Fabriana.

Perhaps she knew that I had not accomplished her mission for her, whatever that mission really was, and was determined that I go back to Skeleton Key.

Perhaps she had realized the risk she had

taken with my life and was ashamed to face me.

Perhaps she couldn't meet me because something terrible had overtaken her.

But I didn't know where she was, how to reach her.

Either I left Key West, and returned home, which was what I wanted most desperately to do, or I returned to the big silver house on the Key, and the ominous currents that seemed to flood it, to face the consequences of what Fabriana might have done.

I knew that common sense and safety suggested the first course. I must leave, forget the Fullers, Mark, Fabriana herself.

Yet I found that I could not.

I must find out what had happened to my sister.

I must find out what threatened her.

I must learn what lay behind the danger of death that clouded Skeleton Key.

I repacked the few things I had brought with me. I brushed the short hair I disliked, and made up my face heavily again. Then, ready as I would ever be, I went back to the office to pay the night's rent for the cottage.

"Your girl friend stood you up, hey?" Enrico asked.

"I imagine she was delayed." I swallowed hard suffocating fear. I went on, "If she comes looking for me tonight, or maybe to-morrow, would you tell her I've gone back to Skeleton Key? Tell her to call me there. Tell her I said she absolutely has to call me there. Okay?"

"Sure. I'll remember to tell her. If she gets here." Enrico eyed me. "You in trouble?"

I shook my head. Then, "Why do you ask?"

"Somebody was here, asking for you. Just a little while ago."

"Who was it?"

Enrico shrugged. "Search me. He said were you staying here? I said you were. He went out. A big tall guy. Dark."

Mark . . .

"What else did he want to know?"

"Nothing."

I thanked Enrico, took my weekend case, and left the motel. I started for the marina, then changed my mind. Karen had mentioned Casey's bar. I would go there first, I decided. Maybe, just maybe, I could find Fabriana.

I was surprised that Mark had come to the Seaside Motel, looking for me, and then gone away without coming back to the cottage. I would ask him about that when I saw him. The detour to Casey's bar wouldn't take me long, I supposed. Mark would surely wait for me at the marina.

I headed toward the lights of Duval Street,

assuming that Casey's bar would be somewhere along it. But I was still surprised when I saw the flickering blue neon that named it.

I hesitated for a moment, uneasily contemplating an entrance alone into a bar I didn't know. Then, determined to see if Fabriana could be there, remembering what Karen had said, I went in.

Fabriana was not at the bar, nor was she sitting in any of the booths that lined the wall.

I turned toward the door, disappointed and disheartened. It opened. Mark came in.

He stared at me through the haze of blue smoke.

"I know you weren't here that night Karen said that she saw you," he said at last. "But what are you doing here now?"

I blinked long lashes at him. I made myself smile. "She got me curious about Casey's. I came to see what it was like."

"Come on," he said in a curt voice. "Let's get back to the launch."

I went with him unwillingly, suddenly afraid.

He hurried me along the street, away from the lights, the people, into the shadows of the lane where the marina was.

He helped me on to the launch. Then, instead of busying himself with the hawsers, the controls, instead of setting out for Skeleton Key, he stood over me. He said, "We have to have a talk."

"We do," I agreed. "Why were you asking for me at the motel?"

"I wanted to know if you were actually there."

"What were you doing at Casey's?"

"The same reason," he answered.

Peculiarly, although I was angry with him, and very suspicious, I was aware of a strange feeling of joy. I was glad to see him. I had left him the night before, certain that I never would lay eyes on him again, never look into his pale narrowed eyes, nor his lean face. I had left him without saying goodbye, somehow sorry that he would never know me. Know Cecily instead of Fabriana.

I cherished the small joy while he stared down into my face.

At last he said, "Fab, you're up to something. And it's something dangerous to you, to others. I'm going to find out what it is."

I felt the blood leave my face, my lips. I felt chill settle on my flesh. The breathless sultry air was suddenly cold.

"It's no use, Fab. I won't let you pretend with me any more."

"I don't know what you're talking about," I said quietly.

"Listen, do you think I'm a fool?" he demanded.

My heart began to beat very hard. He must know the truth. How had he discovered it? Who else knew?

Then he said, "It's the treasure, isn't it? Do you need that terrible tainted gold so much? Are you so greedy that you'll risk your very life for it? Can it matter that much to you?"

My head whirled. My body shook with sudden relief. I wasn't discovered after all. Mark still thought me to be Fabriana. Fabriana herself was safe. Safe for the moment, at least. Wherever she was, whatever she was doing, she was undiscovered, so no one could hurt her.

"Do you think I'm going to let you die for gold?" he was saying.

Perhaps it was the contempt in his voice. Perhaps it was the stress on the word "gold." Perhaps it was simply time. I don't know why it happened then. I'll never know. But that was when a small, long-buried memory surfaced in the form of an image.

I remembered a cheap medallion studded with blue and red stones, a long tarnished chain . . .

The garish display had been on the drug store counter. Fabriana had gone back to it again and again, attracted in some way that I couldn't understand. But I had been half way up the block, and Fabriana said later, "Take this home for me, will you, Cece?" and thrust her lunch box at me before hurrying away. Moments later I'd felt a hand on my shoulder. A gruff angry voice demanded, "Let me have that, kiddo. What do you think you're up to?"

The medallion was there. I saw it and couldn't speak. I couldn't deny his accusation. Though Fabriana could, and did, later on. "I didn't do it, I didn't, I didn't," she'd screamed. "You can't say that I did. It was Cecily. Not me." The man looked from her to me and back again and shrugged. "Well, one of you did, and it was in the lunch box you were carrying," and he pointed his hand at me. I didn't defend myself. I was lectured, and punished of course. For a while I was carefully watched. When we were alone Fabriana wept, "I couldn't help it. I didn't mean to, Cece. But I was scared. I was too scared to admit I'd taken it. I knew you'd be all right. You always know what to do. You're always all right. I just couldn't help it."

Now, wincing under Mark's accusing stare, I knew that poor Fabriana would say the same thing when I faced her down. She would plead that she couldn't help it. She couldn't help wanting the treasure. She couldn't help tricking me into taking her place as target, while she herself plotted her way into wealth. It was so terribly, painfully clear to me now.

Yet what could I say to Mark? How could I betray my sister to him?

"You haven't answered me," he was saying, his voice suddenly gentle now. He went on, "I don't think I really believe it, Fab. I did, you know. Almost from the first. After I came here. I really did believe it of you. I had good reason to. The way you slipped off in the canoe to meet with Hank on the other side of the island. Did you think I didn't find out about that? The way you looked at Dwayne . . . But somehow, in the past couple of weeks . . . I don't know . . . something's changed. I just . . . There's some explanation, isn't there? Won't you tell me what it is?"

Fabriana meeting Hank clandestinely . . .

Her relationship with Dwayne . . .

Her fear . . .

Her determination . . .

But I couldn't tell Mark the truth. I couldn't betray her. Not now. Not yet.

I said, "Mark, there is no treasure. How can you accuse me of trying to . . . to steal something that doesn't exist?"

He smiled faintly. "Are you really going to persuade me you believe that?"

"But I do," I insisted. "Dwayne has said so many times. And he'd know if anyone would."

"Of course. What makes you think he's telling the truth, however?"

"But why shouldn't I believe him, Mark?"

"Because none of the others do. And they were on the dig with him."

"It doesn't make sense. Why should Dwayne lie?"

"I can think of several possibilities. Perhaps he's an idealist, and doesn't want to desecrate a religious site. Even a pagan one."

"It could be that," I agreed. "But somehow . . . "

Mark went on thoughtfully, "And maybe he knows that the treasure can't be removed legally, and he's waiting until after his book comes out, his story of it accepted, before he goes after it illegally."

"That doesn't seem like him," I protested.

"It doesn't seem like you, now, to be involved in a mercenary scheme."

"I'm not," I denied hotly.

"You're in danger, Fab. You've had several close brushes with death in these past weeks. Someone thinks you're very much involved."

"But I'm not," I repeated stubbornly. Then, feeling foolish, but risking it anyway, I asked, "Mark, do you think it could be Mayeroni? Could there be any truth to the legend?"

"I don't know," Mark answered softly. "I just don't know."

I thought of Alice Kane then, and Mickey Hendle. How could what happened to them fit the scheme Mark was suggesting?

I asked him.

He said, "Alice was on the expedition, remember."

And I recalled now that Rosa had said Dwayne was interested in Alice Kane before she died, that Fabriana had tried to come between them in some way.

Alice, working with Dwayne, might have known more about the expedition, about the Mayeroni treasure.

Fabriana would surely have guessed that.

With Alice gone . . .

I stopped the thought before it blossomed. I could not allow myself such ugly speculation.

I said quickly, "But Mark, Dwayne would know, realize, what's behind all this. He'd stop it."

"Would he?"

"Of course."

"Even if he had so much to gain that he couldn't jeopardize it?"

"I don't know," I said disconsolately. Somehow I couldn't imagine Dwayne that way.

"You know him better than I do. After all,

in a year, and with the way he feels about you . . ."

A flush touched my cheeks. I shook my head in childish denial.

"Everybody knows it, Fab. Charlotte and Karen are sitting back, waiting to see him make a fool of himself over a girl more than thirty years younger than he is. He lost his wife seven years ago. Then there was Alice." Sudden bitterness ladled Mark's voice. "And he lost her. So . . ."

I began shakily, "Whatever you think . . ."

"Hank's waiting for you to make your move, too, you know. I expect he wants to see Dwayne taken care of so he can convince Karen to marry him."

Mark had tied it up so neatly. And made Fabriana the culprit. Made me the culprit.

The very neatness increased my suspicion of him. Perhaps it was he who was after Mayeroni's treasure. How could I know, be sure?

"Go away, Fab. Whatever you planned, wanted, is best forgotten," he said.

Was he thinking of me, my safety? Or was he thinking of the treasure?

More than anything then I wanted to do as he urged me. I wanted to step off the launch, turn my back on him, on Skeleton Key forever, on Mayeroni's curse. To bury deep the knowledge of what Fabriana had done to me, the knowledge of the hatred she must bear me.

For it was clear to me now that she had persuaded me to take her place, to be her stand-in and sacrifice, while she herself somehow managed to claim those golden ornaments, those gleaming jewels, she had always desired. She had even told me, when I met her in the Seaside Motel, that she wanted more than anything to have lots of money. I had hardly listened to her then, but I should have.

I was to be her decoy, bear her terror, her pain, perhaps die in her place. Then she, still safe and whole would hold those ornaments in her hands and whisper over those jewels.

There was no longer any question in my mind. I knew that she believed in Mayeroni, in the wealth he guarded. She would do anything to get it.

But if I were to leave now, to disappear, what would happen to her?

Would she be destroyed?

Would she be lost forever?

I knew that I could never go away, not until I had spoken to her, pleaded with her to save herself. I knew that I had to wait.

At last, instead of replying directly to Mark's urgent plea that I go away, I said, "It's time for us to get back."

"Then you won't listen to me?"

"I can't."

"Even though you know what risks you're taking?"

I shivered, asked, "Is that a veiled threat, Mark?"

"I'm asking you to save yourself," he retorted.

"Thank you for your concern," I said coldly. And then, "Or is that what it is?"

He didn't answer me. He busied himself at the controls, cast off, and directed the launch across the darkness of the cove.

He didn't speak until we heard the toll of the buoys, and he was steering carefully between their intermittent lights through the narrow channel that cut the reefs. Then, very quietly, he said, "Be careful, very careful, from now on, Fabriana."

Chapter 11

"And how is your friend?" Karen asked, a sly grin turning her lips.

She sat primly on the sofa, a half-finished drink in her slender hand. Her open-necked silk shirt made her throat seem long and slim.

I thought of the portrait of her mother. Caroline's throat had been long and slim, too. Caroline's faint smile had had a quality of slyness.

I reminded myself that Caroline Fuller had been dead for seven years. I mustn't divert myself with speculation about her. I answered Karen as casually as I could, saying, "My friend didn't show up. So I don't really know what's going on now. But I expect she's all right. Otherwise I would probably have heard."

Dwayne raised his brows and leaned forward, his scored face earnest, "Fabriana, you know what I think? When your friend gets in touch with you again, you ought to invite her out here to stay. There's no need for you to rush into town to meet her. We have plenty of room, and it would be easier on you, wouldn't it?"

Karen chuckled. "Dad, you can be so naive. Maybe Fabriana has her reasons for going into town. Maybe she gets tired of us."

Hank cut in then, "Why don't you speak for yourself, Karen? I have the feeling that you're the one that gets tired."

She shot him a quick narrow-eyed look, "I didn't ask you what your feelings were, Hank."

He was plainly unperturbed by her snappishness. He shrugged his wide shoulders, grinned, "One of these days you'll make up your mind. Until then, I'll keep hoping."

She blushed, didn't answer.

Charlotte said testily, "It seems to me that lovers' quarrels, if that's what the two of you are engaging in, ought to be carried on in private. Not be held as open forums where everyone in the family, and out of it, too, has to listen and observe."

Karen jerked gracelessly to her feet. "You always have something to say, haven't you, Charlotte? Well, you can't fool me. It's not my welfare, nor my love affairs that concern you!"

Dwayne rose. He divided a placating look between Charlotte and Karen, then said, "Oh, come on, what's a bit of teasing between aunt and niece?"

"You should mind your own business," Karen spat at him. "You're in no position to tease anyone." Her narrowed, too-bright eyes were fixed on me, I saw.

Charlotte turned on him, too. She said, "As for suggesting that Fabriana should bring some stranger here . . . What are you thinking of, Dwayne? Don't we already have enough trouble to contend with?" Her voice dropped to a whisper. "Mayeroni waits. He listens. The old wickedness is alive, ready to strike again."

Dwayne's big brown hands became fists on his knees, but he didn't answer.

They had all been waiting for me, I knew, waiting for my return.

Now that I was here the tension had overflowed.

I didn't know what to say.

I didn't want to hurt them.

I wouldn't hurt them.

But how could I reassure them without betraying Fabriana?

As soon as I dared, I excused myself, saying I was tired and would go to bed.

Mark went with me into the patio.

I turned my head away as we passed the statue of Mayeroni. But I thought that I felt those terrible sightless eyes follow me through the shadows.

"They're on edge, aren't they?" Mark said.

I didn't answer him.

"It's because you've come back," he said softly. "You know that, don't you? They're scared, because you've come back."

Alone in the comfortable room I had thought I would never see again, I paced the floor. I was convinced now that Fabriana must have believed that there was a treasure to be found, that Dwayne Fuller had located it, and was, for reasons of his own, hiding it. Either one, or more, of the others, also were certain of that and had tried to remove the threat of Fabriana from Skeleton Key. So Fabriana had called me in, and disappeared. But she would be nearby. She must be, for Karen had seen her in Casey's bar and mistaken her for me.

What did my twin plan?

How would she return, and when?

Who was prepared to kill her to keep her from discovering the treasure Dwayne had discovered?

Was it Mark? Was that why he persisted in warning me that I was in danger?

Could it be Karen? She so plainly didn't like me, considered me somehow a rival for Hank's affections. Had she tampered with the wardrobe, the canoe? Had she placed the ground glass in the orange juice for which Rosa had been blamed?

It occurred to me then that Charlotte might only be pretending to believe in the Mayeroni curse. She had been on the expedition. Perhaps she knew or hoped to know where the treasure was, wanted it for herself, for Dwayne.

Hank seemed the least concerned of any of them. Was that an act? He had, by Mark's account, often met Fabriana on the other side of the island. Had they been working together? Then why had he given me no sign, spoken no revealing word to me? Or was he simply a fortune-hunter, hoping to marry Karen for her income, and taking no sides to avoid endangering his position with her?

Dwayne insisted there was no Mayeroni treasure. Could he simply be waiting, as Mark had suggested, to bring it out of Yucatan illegally? Was he determined to conceal its whereabouts until he was able safely to do that?

I felt lost in the sea of bewildering possibilities. Yet I didn't feel that I could give up. I couldn't abandon Fabriana, no matter what she had done.

I was determined to save myself, to save her, too.

I thought of the manuscript Dwayne was working on. Perhaps if I were to read it again, to study it, I could find within it the clue that I needed.

I looked outside. A light still burned in Mark's room.

I hurried to his door, knocked.

He called out, "Come in."

He was at his desk, the manuscript before him, yellow under a pool of white light.

I wondered suddenly if he, too, was studying what Dwayne had written, what he himself had rewritten, in search of a clue to understanding.

"I thought . . ." I hesitated. Then, "I thought, if you didn't need the script, I would do over some of the corrected sheets tonight."

"If you want to . . ." He gathered the script together, slid it to the edge of the desk. "Help yourself. But isn't it rather late?"

I didn't answer. I took the script, turned to go.

"I never knew you to look for work before," he told me softly.

A strange hush seemed to hang over Skeleton Key, over the sun-silvered house that sprawled beneath the palms.

In that next week I felt as if I were always holding my breath, and sensed that all the others felt much the same way.

There was no name to give the uneasiness that pervaded all of us. But whatever it was, it kept Dwayne from working. He walked about, pacing restlessly from room to room, passing Mayeroni without a glance, to disappear into the grounds for hours on end.

Charlotte and Karen bickered irritably with each other, while Hank maintained his boyish charm, and a superficial calm, though he was plainly as stirred up as the others.

Mark was watchful, quiet, and it seemed, ever present.

Rosa muttered that Mayeroni had pushed himself into all their lives and that no one was safe from him, nor would anyone ever be, until his angry ghost was laid for good.

I felt as if I were walking a shivering tightrope over the pit of imminent death. I thought there must be another attempt on me soon. I couldn't see from which direction, from whom, it would come. I couldn't imagine how I could prevent it.

I didn't know where Fabriana was, what she was doing.

I didn't know when I would hear from her.

The small shuttered cottage in which I had done my painting, in which I had lived so pleasantly, seemed part of a far away and long lost world now. I began to wonder if I would ever see it again. I began to wonder if I would hear Mr. Pierce's whistle and rush to the door to chat with him, while he handed me my mail.

Towards the end of the week, I was sitting near the window overlooking the green lawn.

I heard Karen say, in a voice drawing closer, "Oh, Hank, why do you keep pushing at me? I don't know what I want to do. When I do know I'll tell you. I promise, I'll tell you. Isn't that good enough?"

"I guess it'll have to be," he answered. "But I don't see why you keep stalling me. What's the use of waiting? You're a big girl. You ought to know what you want. You ought to know if you're stuck on your father or if you're willing to settle for me."

"That's disgusting," she retorted. "It's not a choice between the two of you. You're just trying to make me angry. But I won't let you. It's just that I don't know what Dad will say. We've been together, you know. Together for so long. Why, ever since my mother died . . ."

"Of course you know. He'll say good luck. He won't mind being turned loose. He's got his eyes on somebody else."

"Somebody else? What are you talking about?"

Even before he replied, I knew what his

190

words would be. I bit my lip angrily, tempted to fling the window open more widely. To let the others know I could hear them.

Hank's answer was, "You know as well as I do that your father is crazy about Fabriana. If it weren't for you, and for Charlotte, of course, he'd do something about it."

"You're out of your mind," Karen retorted. "I don't believe you."

Hank laughed, unperturbed as always. "Okay, I'm out of my mind."

"You're not going to stampede me that way," Karen cried shakily. "He needs me. He always has. You can't make me turn against him with your ugly ideas."

"What's so ugly about it?" Hank demanded. "A man needs a woman, Karen. He wants love in his life. What's wrong with him taking love where he finds it."

"My father's different. He's not like you, like other men." She stopped. Then, "Besides, he's got me, hasn't he? He doesn't need anybody else."

"It isn't quite the same thing. You're his daughter," Hank told her.

She didn't answer him. She made a small angry sound that was part grunt, part moan.

I heard her go stamping away in her field boots, boots like those her mother had worn for the portrait in the dining room.

I wondered why Hank had spoken like that to Karen. It seemed an odd way to press his suit.

But I wondered, too, why Karen seemed to vacillate between wanting Hank and turning away from him. It was as if she couldn't quite make up her mind which way she wanted to go.

Rosa interrupted my thoughts. She peered in at me, her dark eyes alight with mischief. "You've got a phone call in the library. Maybe it's that friend of yours. The one you meet in Key West."

"I hope so," I muttered, and hurried along with her back to the library. She opened the door for me. I ran across the room to the table. But I waited until she had closed the door behind her before I picked up the phone. When I was sure that I was alone, I said, "Yes. Who is it?"

A small breathless silence lay on the humming wires.

Fabriana? Could it be she? Then why didn't she answer? Why didn't she speak?

"Yes," I repeated. "Who is it? Who do you want?"

"You. You're the one I want."

It was Fabriana's voice, her faint laughter.

"Why didn't you meet me when you were supposed to?" I demanded. "What do you

192

think you've accomplished by . . . " Suddenly I stopped. It was true that I was alone, but how did I know who might be listening on any of the numerous extension phones in the house.

I said, "Look, I have to see you. Shall we meet in the usual place? Just name the day."

"Have you done anything for me?"

"Listen. There's nothing I can do." I tried to load my voice with meaning, to make her understand without putting anything into words. "You don't realize what's been going on. I have to talk to you about it. I won't . . . "

"We'll get together soon," Fabriana whispered. "Just sit tight."

"No. That's just what I can't do. I'm afraid you don't understand. You have to give me a chance to talk to you."

"Oh, yes," Fabriana laughed. "Never mind. Just hang on a little longer. It'll soon be all right."

I cried, "Wait. Don't . . . "

But I realized almost immediately that I was speaking into a dead phone. Fabriana had hung up. She was gone. She was gone as if she had never spoken to me, gone without promising to meet me. Then why had she called? What had she intended to say?

I leaned against the table. I felt a beading of perspiration on my upper lip. I felt the pulse begin to beat in my throat. My hands shook as I brushed my bangs from my forehead.

Why hadn't I told her that I was leaving?

Why hadn't I said I would no longer take part in the deception that was part of whatever she was planning?

And Mark said from the doorway, "Something wrong, Fab? Bad news? You're white as a sheet."

Before I could think, control myself, I had turned on him angrily. I demanded, "Are you following me around, Mark? Were you eavesdropping on me?"

"Oh, I do beg your pardon," he retorted coldly. "I came in here because I was passing in the hall and I heard your voice. I didn't intend to eavesdrop. And I didn't. You had already hung up by the time I opened the door. But I did hear you and I thought you sounded upset."

I forced myself to smile. "I guess I was. If I accuse you so foolishly, then I am upset. But it's nothing really." I went to the door, started to edge past him.

His big hand fell on my shoulder. "Just a minute, Fab. Who was it? What did they want? Why are you so pale?"

"It was my friend, the one I met in Key West weeks ago, and didn't meet the last time I went in. She *did* rather upset me. Because, I guess, she's upset herself, and then, before she'd explained, she hung up."

"Then call her back," he suggested.

"I'm afraid that I don't know where to reach her."

He took a deep breath, let it out slowly. "I think, if I were you, Fab, I'd shake myself loose of her. She seems like a troublemaker to me. There are people like that, you know. People who use you, and end up hurting you. The only way to handle them is to give them a wide berth. Even if you care deeply about them."

"Thanks for the advice," I said, smiling sweetly. "I'll try to keep it in mind."

But I wondered who he was thinking about.

Did he know about Fabriana, about me?

Or, when he said those words, had he been remembering Alice Kane?

He gave me a hard, angry stare. "You little fool, do you think that I'm playing games with you?"

"Not games," I answered. "No, not games. But something. Yes. I think you're playing something."

Before he could answer me, I went back to my room, glad of the prospect of a few hours respite.

It seemed to me that I would not be able much longer to force myself through conversations that were increasingly frightening, increasingly meaningless. It seemed to me that what Fabriana had asked of me was impossible. I could not unravel the evil web in which she had found herself. I no longer wanted to. I wanted only to find an escape that would leave Fabriana unharmed.

I sat down at the desk, my head in my hands.

I felt adrift, frightened, unable, for the first time in my life, to see the right step ahead, to know what to do, and how to do it.

I supposed that now I understood Fabriana better than I had ever understood my twin before. The thought was even more frightening. Was I, in playing Fabriana's part, taking over her personality, too? Was I exposing myself to forces over which I would soon have no control?

Something touched my arm, fuzzy, scratchy, infinitely unpleasant. I brushed my hand against it, not looking at it.

But, on the floor, in the pale glow of the lamp, there was a sudden shadow. A dark blot, crisp and clear, showed against the tan of the rug.

It hunched, moved, furry and black, quick as an indrawn breath. It skittered awkwardly toward my feet.

I jumped back, screaming soundlessly, my

throat raw with the ache of restraint, my lungs freezing with compacted breath.

I caught up the wad of papers on the desk, and slammed it down as hard as I could.

The black blot lunged for the shadow of the chair beneath me.

I hurled myself up, and away, and into the dark of the patio.

Chapter 12

The door slammed shut behind me. The sound cracked like a pistol shot through the stillness.

Instantly a light flashed on in Mark's room. Almost immediately Dwayne's window glowed.

I waited, trying to collect my scattered wits. But my flesh seemed to crawl. I felt as if a million insects had lit upon me to nibble and gnaw.

Mark reached me first. "What is it?" he demanded.

I could only shake my head, point toward the closed door of my room. I tried to control the trembling that swept me, telling myself that I was too grown up to respond to such childish and primitive emotions.

Dwayne came then. He was breathless, panting. His face was tinged with a greenish pallor in the pale lights that poured from the rooms.

He put his arms around me, drew me close.

I could feel the heave of his chest, the beat of his heart. "Fabriana?" he asked. "What happened?"

The patio globes suddenly spilled brilliance on us.

Karen ambled toward me, tying her robe around her, and yawning. "What's all the noise about?" she complained. "Can't we ever get a night's sleep around here?"

Charlotte, two steps behind her, moaned, "You know what it is, Karen. You know, too, Dwayne. It's Mayeroni. None of you will listen to me, but you'll all see. I know. I know."

Mark had given me a long considering look, a look that acknowledged the presence of Dwayne's arms around me, I realized. He had turned, gone into my room before I could manage a protest.

Now he came out, shaking his head. "There's nobody inside. There's nothing inside."

Close by, shaking his head from side to side in amused disbelief, Hank asked, "What did you expect?"

I wet my dry lips, whispered, "I saw a spider. Big, fuzzy, black. It was waiting for me on my desk. It was just sitting there, waiting, I tell you, and I disturbed it."

Karen gave a hoot of laughter. "Oh, you idiot! You've been here a whole year and you don't even know a palmetto bug when you see one."

"Are you sure it was a spider?" Dwayne asked.

"I'm sure."

"Then let's have a look," he said breathlessly.

His arms dropped away from me, much to my relief.

He went toward my room, moving very slowly, breathing hard, and when his face passed under the light, it showed faint tinges of green again.

"I," Karen snapped, "do not intend to go looking for palmetto bugs, nor spiders, either real or imaginary."

"But I saw it," I cried. "It was so . . . ugly. So predatory looking."

"Like some people, I suppose," Karen retorted. She shrugged, linked her arm through Hank's. "Come along, darling. Fabriana's already proved that she has more lives than a cat, don't you think?"

"That's really quite unkind of you," Charlotte cried. "If you'd found a spider in your room, you'd expect someone to help you."

"I proved very well on the dig that I don't need anybody's help," Karen answered. "And you know that perfectly well. If you won't admit it, then I'm sure that my father will."

Dwayne, at the door by then, turned back. "Oh, yes," he said gently. "But that has

200

nothing to do with now." He went on to me, "Could it have been a black widow, Fabriana?"

"Maybe. I'm not sure. I didn't dare touch it. But that's what I thought. So I jumped back and it skittered away. And I ran."

"We'll see if we can find it," he said, and disappeared inside.

I leaned against the wall, still shivering. I wondered what to do, wondered what I could do. Was this one of those natural things that could happen in the Key West climate, where all sorts of insects abounded? Or was this one more deliberate attack on me? Finally I sank to the steps.

Charlotte sat down beside me. "Fabriana, I wish you would listen."

I turned, studied her suddenly gaunt, shadowed face.

She went on, "Remember, when you first came here, you heard me saying that no good would come out of that business in Yucatan. That was before anything happened, wasn't it?"

I nodded.

"I had my reasons, you know. I felt that you should understand. I spoke to you, just as I first spoke to Alice Kane. Neither of you paid any attention to me. But you see, it wasn't just Mayeroni. It was Karen, too. She was so determined to be the beginning and the end to Dwayne. And, of course, she couldn't. Nobody could. Ever since Caroline died in that terrible accident, Dwayne's only been part of a man. Though that's a cruel way of putting it. What I'm trying to say is . . . "

It was just then that I heard Mark's exclamation.

I scrambled to my feet.

Dwayne was saying, "Wait. Careful. Let me have a look."

I pressed my nose against the window, peering inside.

Dwayne and Mark were bent over the rug together.

Mark moved a pencil.

The black blot flipped over, struggled.

"Yes," Mark muttered.

Dwayne slammed a heavy pad folded double into the rug. The black blot was still. He got to his feet heavily.

I knew I was safe then, safe for the moment.

I opened the door, went inside. I didn't have to ask what Dwayne and Mark had found.

But Dwayne said heavily, "It was a black widow. But it's dead now."

"They turn up around here, don't they, sometimes, Dwayne?" Mark asked.

"Sometimes." His blue lips turned in a false smile. "You can forget all about it, Fabriana. The two great white hunters have destroyed it."

But, when I was at last alone again, I wondered if I dared forget it.

Had the black widow found its way into the room by accident? Could it have hidden in any other room? Or had it been carefully brought here, either to frighten me, or when disturbed, to have bitten, poisoned me?

Was this one more attack on me, on Fabriana?

Or was it one more unexplainable accident?

"Recovered from your ordeal of last night?" Karen asked. She smiled over her grapefruit, then spooned up a mouthful.

She seemed more friendly than usual that morning, as if to make amends for her so obvious lack of sympathy the night before.

But I knew that might not be the reason. Karen could have completely forgotten my experience with the spider. She had, I had learned, a way of blowing hot and cold. It occurred to me that she might never know herself how she would feel from one moment to the next.

I didn't have to answer her.

Hank came into the dining room. He sat

down, spread a grin between Karen and me. "Something seems to be going on. Have you seen Dwayne today?"

Karen shook her head.

"No," I said. "What is it?"

"I'm not sure. But he's sitting at poolside, looking grim. I haven't seen him like that since the packers forgot half the equipment, and he had to wait two days alone while the rest of us went back and got it."

"You naturally think that's terribly amusing, don't you?" Karen snapped. "You don't know what he has on his mind. Maybe it's something serious." Her voice grew spiteful. "Serious enough to affect you and me. Not that you'd care."

"You know better, Karen. I care about anything that affects you. And me. That's exactly it. That's why I mentioned it. I thought maybe you, or you, Fabriana, would know what's going on."

I shook my head.

Karen said, "I'll go and find out." She slanted a look at me. "Maybe he's wondering about your fit last night." She pushed back her chair, stamped out through the tiled hallway, her boots trailing echoes behind her.

The phone rang once. Then stopped.

I waited hopefully. Perhaps it was Fabriana. Perhaps, now, I could talk to her.

Moments later Rosa brought the silver coffee urn into the dining room.

I eyed her expectantly, but she said nothing.

It was Hank that asked, "Didn't I hear the phone just now?"

"It was a wrong number," she answered absently.

When she had left us, Hank raised his brows at me, grinned, "Dwayne doesn't look like a man stuck on his book. And I don't think that's what's troubling him."

"Is that so?" I asked, as carefully non-committal as I could be.

"Exactly so." Hank paused. "I'd say he was a man trying to make up his mind between two unsatisfactory choices."

"But about what?"

Hank shrugged.

I had the feeling that he was warning me. There was no real clue in what he was saying, except that it could be taken so many ways. It could mean that Hank was telling me, that he, maybe Dwayne, too, knew I was not Fabriana. If so, why didn't Hank come right out and say it? Why was he just hinting?

Or was I imagining the significant heaviness in his voice? Was my own sense of guilt deceiving me?

"I'm going into town for a few hours this

afternoon," Hank said. "Anything you want me to get for you?"

"I can't think of anything."

"I'd suggest you come along, if you want, but I'm going to be doing a lot of small errands. You wouldn't enjoy it."

"I think I'd better stay here," I answered.

Moments later, Karen returned. She slumped in the seat, frowning deeply. "It's no use. I can't talk to him. Not any more. We used to be so close. We used to be able to read each other's minds almost. He told me everything, and I told him everything. Ever since my mother died, it was like that. I didn't think it could change. But it's all gone now. It's as if we're nothing to each other any more." Her eyes brushed Hank, touched me. "He wouldn't even say what he was worrying about. He wouldn't even let me help him. And it's so obvious that he does need help."

"We'll find out soon enough," Hank told her. "If you couldn't get it from him, then you couldn't. Don't worry. When he wants to he'll let you, and the rest of us, know what's going on."

I rose, excused myself. As I went toward the door, the portrait of Karen's mother caught my eye again. I kept picturing it as I went on into the tiled hallway. Karen's resemblance to her mother was so strong. But I dismissed that. I wondered suddenly why Dwayne had never married again. Caroline had been dead for seven years. He was surely young enough to need the love and companionship of a wife. Though he had Karen, and Charlotte, they could hardly fill the void left by widowerhood. It was one more question I couldn't answer.

I shrugged, went into the patio, and crossed to the pool.

Dwayne was peering into its blue depths. He looked up at my approach. He said, "I've been waiting for you. We need to have a talk. Will you come along to my office where we won't be disturbed?"

"Of course," I said. "But you haven't had any breakfast yet. Wouldn't you like some coffee first? Or shall I ask Rosa to bring a tray to your desk?"

He rubbed his chest, and sighed. There was a strange note in his voice when he said, "Perhaps later on, Fabriana. But not now."

There was something odd, too, in the way his blue eyes did not quite meet mine.

I was suddenly uneasy.

He rose heavily, sighed again. He led the way to his office.

Mark intercepted us. "Okay this morning, Fab?"

I nodded.

He turned to Dwayne. "What about to-day's work?"

"I don't have anything for you. You can go ahead with the polishing up of what you've got."

"I have a suggestion," Mark said. "You might find that if you dictated into a tape recorder, just talked what you wanted to say, you might get yourself started again."

"I might," Dwayne agreed. "But I'm not interested at the moment. I'll think about it later on. In a day or so we'll know where we stand."

Mark seemed to want to say more, but Dwayne rubbed his chest, sighed, then went on. I followed him.

I looked back when we reached the office door.

Mark was standing where we had left him, still watching us.

Dwayne ushered me inside, closed the door gently.

A pulse began to beat hard in my throat. I was sure that I knew what was coming. I braced myself for it. I began, even, to pick and choose my words.

He set a chair for me, and waved me into it.

Then he took the big swivel behind the desk, and sat back, regarding me silently.

The light was on my face. The bright sun

was blinding. It made a dark still silhouette of him. A form that was all shadow, faceless and expressionless.

He let the silence go on for so long a time that my alarm grew to such proportions I was afraid I would not be able to conceal it for long.

But at last, he said quietly, "I thought that you knew, Fabriana, that you understood. These last weeks have been so difficult, I can understand so well that they would affect you. But I didn't believe they could change you."

Panic, mixed with joyful relief, swept me.

He knew. He knew.

It was over now.

I opened my lips to speak.

He raised his hand. "Wait, Fabriana. Just listen to me. Don't be ashamed. Don't deny it. I don't blame you. I felt it last night. When you were so frightened, and I held you in my arms . . . I knew then that I'd hurt you. You no longer trusted me. I'm sorry. I never meant it to be that way. It was for you, for you, Fabriana. I had to wait, think. I had to decide what to do."

I realized, then, that I had been wrong. His was not the face of a man about to accuse me. Not the voice of a man about to indict me or expose me.

I tried to stop him, but once again he silenced me with a small gesture.

He went on, "When I lost my wife, lost Caroline, I felt that my life had ended. We had been very close. It was a marriage not like so many in these times. We did everything together, went everywhere together. She was with me on all my expeditions, working shoulder to shoulder with me. She was with me when I did the reports that described my finds. I thought I couldn't go on when she died in that terrible automobile accident. I was a young man then. Perhaps not so young to you, from your perspective. But forty-eight seems hardly in prime to me. But I was lucky. I had Karen. I had my daughter to live for. So I had to go on. She, and Charlotte, too, tried to fill up the emptiness for me, but a daughter, a sister, can never be a wife, you know. The years went by so coldly, but I managed. When I met Alice Kane, and during the time we were in Yucatan, I began to feel that I had something to look forward to after all. She was very bright, gay, a talented woman, an interesting woman."

He paused, and I found myself suddenly remembering the sound of Mark's voice when he spoke of Alice. The love in his voice.

I forced my concentration back to Dwayne. I realized that he was watching me thoughtfully.

I felt the pulse begin to beat in my throat. I said quickly, "Dwayne, please . . . "

He went on as if he hadn't heard me, or refused to acknowledge my pleas. He said, "But someone else was here, too, a beautiful and a very bright girl, a very young girl, of course. But still, a man like myself, accustomed to loving, found it very easy to love her." He stopped, swallowed so painfully that I could see his Adam's apple move in his throat. "It is extraordinary how much room there is in a human being's heart for love, how much he can need, how many times, if he's fortunate, he can find it."

I licked my dry lips, dreading what was to come.

Dwayne said, in a voice suddenly rough, "You must be wondering why I'm telling all this to you, Fabriana."

I simply looked at him. There was nothing to say.

"It's because you don't know. I realize that you can't possibly know." He stopped. He drew a slow ragged breath. "I know," he said. "I know. It sounds as if I'm losing my mind. These past few weeks I've often thought that I might be. Fabriana knew it all. She had been ready to accept me, ready to love me. She understood that I was afraid for her. She realized that I didn't know what to do but that

211

I would try. She knew I would try for her."

"Dwayne," I whispered. "No, please, don't . . ."

A wave of color swept his face, then receded. It left greenish pallor staining his mahogany skin. He said quietly, "You're not Fabriana, are you? You look like her. You speak like her. But you're not her."

It was a moment before I could find breath, and speech. I sat very still, struggling to retain the composure that threatened to seep away from me. He had been wounded beyond belief, and humiliated beyond acceptance, by my betrayal, by Fabriana's betrayal. I had to allow him the dignity of knowing why. I waited until I was quite sure that my voice would be steady, my words clear, and then I said, "Dwayne, I'm sorry. You're right, of course. I'm not Fabriana."

Strangely, though he had plainly demanded, been expecting, my admission, he stared at me in cold disbelief. He asked, "Then who are you? What's the meaning of this . . . this charade you've engaged in?"

"I'm Cecily Harden," I said. "Fabriana's twin sister. We are absolutely alike physically. I *did* have to cut my hair to match hers, and I have used more makeup than usual, because that's *her* way. But otherwise, in voice and speech and form, in every observable way, we're duplicates of each other."

His bluish lips compressed. He rubbed his chest with his bunched fist. He sighed deeply. Then, "Yes. In every observable way. But there must be some difference. Because I sensed something from almost the first time I saw you. Strange little things . . . I don't know quite what it was that caught my attention in the beginning. You don't laugh as much as Fabriana does. You're not as outgoing. Then, one day you did that sketch of Hank . . . Fabriana had never done that. You swam so well Mark told me. You asked questions that Fabriana would never have asked." He breathed deeply. "All right. I realized it finally. Now I want you to explain to me why you are doing this. What it means. Why Fabriana ran away and sent you to take her place."

"She was frightened," I said simply. "She said that she needed my help. I couldn't refuse her. Dwayne, I'm sorry. I wish now . . . I wish with all my heart that I had . . . "

"Frightened," he said in a lifeless voice.

I went back to the very beginning. It was no question now of betraying Fabriana. Dwayne deserved the truth. He had a right to it. I described the letter I had had, and everything that had followed thereafter.

He listened, nodding silently.

213

I ended, "And now I don't know what to do. I'm afraid. For myself. For her, too."

Dwayne said, "I trusted her. Completely and all the way." He was still for a moment, his bluish lips moving silently. Then he went on, "The treasure? No, no. Mayeroni died three hundred years ago. But hatred still lives . . ." He gave me a long sad look. "I loved her, you know. Or is it you, could it be you, that I've begun to love?"

"I'll leave, Dwayne. If you want me to," I said breathlessly, hoping that he would agree and free me. "You have the right to tell me to go. In spite of Fabriana . . ."

"I think not," he answered softly. "We'd better say nothing to the others. We'd better go on as we did before."

Chapter 13

When I finally left him, he was slumped in the chair, his head back, his eyes closed. The pallor of his skin, the droop of his heavy shoulders, made him seem much older now.

I had protested that I saw no reason now to continue the masquerade. I wanted no part of whatever it was that Fabriana planned. I told him so.

"I realize that," he answered. "I have my reasons."

"But what reasons?" I demanded.

He didn't reply. Instead, he told me heavily, "You have nothing to be afraid of any more."

I was shaken by what he had told me, and more so by what he asked. Yet, having tried to trick him, having, in a way, betrayed his trust, I felt obliged to do as he asked. He had the right to expect me to cooperate with him. I wished that he had explained, but I supposed that he had the right to keep his secrets, too.

I closed the door gently behind me, and

turned, and very nearly stumbled over Hank.

He was down on his hands and knees, fiddling with the sprinkler system.

His green eyes glinted with amusement as he slanted an upward glance at me. "Did you get a chewing out? Or what? You look almost as grim as the great Dwayne himself."

I wondered instantly if he had been just below the window, listening while Dwayne and I spoke.

I studied Hank's open bronze face, but couldn't tell if he had really been a third party, unseen and unknown, to that very private conversation. I couldn't tell if now Hank, too, knew that I was not Fabriana.

I said finally, "No. Not exactly, we were talking about the book."

"Oh, were you?" Hank's disbelieving grin was an open challenge.

"I thought you were going in to town this morning," I offered, in a too-obvious attempt to change the subject.

Hank wouldn't have it. His grin widened. He said, "I had the idea he might be proposing to you."

Color swept into my face. I shrugged impatiently. "Well, he didn't. Not that it's any of your business."

"Anything that affects Karen is my business," he retorted. He rose to his feet, kicked the sprinkler aside, and dusted his hands. Then he said, "Then I figured maybe he'd give you the definitive word on Mayeroni."

"Oh, Hank," I said disgustedly.

"You're still a disbeliever, aren't you?"

I shivered although the sun, peculiarly pale and hazy now, was still remarkably hot.

Could the ancient curse of a long-dead man reach out from the grave, across hundreds of years, and thousands of miles? Could the statue in the small patio invoke such powers to protect what it considered its own?

Or was there here, as I somehow thought more probable, even wanted to believe, a human agency at work?

The wardrobe's partly cut legs . . . the concealed tear in the canoe . . . the black widow spider . . . The very nature of these events led me to suspect a hating heart concealed behind smiling lips.

And yet . . . ?

"If you'd been there, seen the place itself, you might better understand how Charlotte feels. If you'd heard the old men talking, hunched over the fires at night . . ."

"Charlotte?" I asked. "What about you?"

He laughed, didn't answer.

Something seemed to amuse him inordinately. I didn't know what it was. Faint curiosity stirred under my annoyance. I blurted,

"I don't think I know you at all." And added hastily, suddenly aware of the mistake I was making. "At least not very well. Considering how long I've known you."

The amusement faded from his face. It turned stony. "Be careful, *Fabriana*," he told me. "Don't commit yourself too far to anything."

I heard the faint stress on the name. It struck me then that I could be sure he had eavesdropped on Dwayne and me. He knew the truth. He must know now that I was not Fabriana, and was warning me that I had almost given myself away. Almost forgotten the role I had promised first my twin, then Dwayne, that I would play.

I managed a light laugh, said, "I suppose people never know each other."

"Sensible girl," he approved.

"Tête-à-tête?" Karen asked, hip-swinging her way down the path to join us. She slipped a possessive arm under Hank's. "Aren't you going canoeing today?" she asked me.

I grimaced, "You know I haven't done that since the day I got into trouble. I don't intend to start again."

"Poor Fabriana . . ." Karen shrugged. Then, to Hank, "I think I'll go in to Key West with you."

He hesitated, then said, "Okay. If you want

to. But it won't be much fun dragging around with me."

"Then we can split up. You go your way, and I'll go mine. We can meet at the launch later."

"I think you'd better stay here, Karen." Hank's voice was flat, empty. He went on, "With the way things are, I mean. I don't like the looks of your father."

"I don't much either. But he won't let me help. So what good can I do?"

"You could be available in case he wants you," Hank said easily. He glanced sideways at me, "The way Fabriana will be." Smiling now, Hank added, "And that's at some sacrifice to her, too. Dwayne's had her in there on the carpet. I would guess she's had a bellyful of the Fullers today."

Karen grinned nastily. "I doubt that. If she had, she'd be busy packing."

"I have no reason to," I told her, hoping that I sounded more convincing than I felt.

I had every reason to flee Skeleton Key.

I felt as if the tightrope over the pit of death on which I so gingerly walked was shivering more and more. I felt that the shadow of Mayeroni was growing larger and larger, and falling more heavily on me. I sensed that the animosity of the others toward me was growing, too. I didn't know how long I could manage to wear Fabriana's face, maintain the veneer of Fabriana's personality over the very real terror that I myself felt.

I was relieved when Mark joined us, saying, "Rosa's hovering over the luncheon table with rage on her face. If we don't let her serve us now, we may be out the best housekeeper and cook anybody ever had."

Hank walked with us toward the dining room, then said that he would go in to town.

Mark squinted at the hazy sky. "If you are, then you'd better plan on getting back fairly early, I think. I've heard that the barometer's falling. There are storm warnings out. Something that was simmering over Cuba for a few days is heading this way on the boil."

"Maybe you shouldn't go, Hank," Karen suggested.

"I'll be back in plenty of time." He left us without giving her time to answer him.

As we went into the house, I heard the sound of the launch fading away across the cove. He had wasted no time in getting started.

I wondered what his errands were.

He had plainly not wanted company with him.

He had discouraged first me, then Karen, from going along.

I made up my mind to get a good look at him when he returned.

Charlotte was waiting in the dining room.

Rosa danced on impatient feet beside her, but as soon as we entered, the plump doll-like woman bustled away to the kitchen.

"What about Dwayne?" Charlotte frowned.

"He told me he wouldn't be in," Mark said.

"Is he all right?" Charlotte demanded, thrusting her chair back, her pretty face all angles of concern.

Karen sighed, "Why don't you stop mothering him, Charlotte? My own mother never did. She hated the very idea of it. I never do either. I think it's disgusting that you should baby him when he's a grown man, and years older than you are."

Charlotte sank back in her chair. Patches of color bloomed on her cheekbones. Her eyes flashed. "You don't know what it means to have affection for anyone," she answered coldly. She turned to Mark. "Is he ill? Why doesn't he want lunch?"

Mark seemed to ponder his answer. Then, "He didn't say. My guess is that he's distracted." His pale eyes moved to brush me. "You talked to him, Fabriana. What do you think?"

"Why . . . why, I don't know," I stammered. "I thought . . . he seemed . . . " I let it go finally, not knowing how to finish.

Rosa thrust her way through the swinging

doors. She served us cold chicken salad and hot bread and huge platters of sliced melon.

When she had gone, Charlotte said hopefully, "Maybe he's getting ready to start working again."

"Possibly," Karen agreed. "He does always get that distracted look when he's ready to go on."

"Then he'll finish the book soon," Charlotte said.

But I knew that what was troubling Dwayne now was not the book. His thoughts, like mine, were with Fabriana.

He had said he had trusted Fabriana, trusted her, and loved her. He said that he had needed her.

But in these past weeks, since I had taken her place on Skeleton Key, he must have been gravely shaken in his feelings. The differences he had sensed must have troubled and bewildered him. They must have frightened him, as he grew more certain each day that the Fabriana he had known was gone and another had come to take her place. I had seen the stricken gray look on his face when I admitted the deception, seen it deepen as I explained.

I had trembled with fear, yes, but with relief, too.

But he had been hurt, hurt, and more than that, I understood now. He had been frightened as well.

But of what he was frightened, I wasn't sure.

I knew only that it must have something to do with the attacks on Fabriana, the attacks that had driven her away, leaving me in her place, the attacks that had continued, worsened, as if I were Fabriana.

Did he know who was behind them?

Did he know why one of the people on the island wanted to see Fabriana dead?

Was it Charlotte? Mark? Hank? Karen? Or was it Dwayne himself?

Was he hiding behind the Mayeroni myth? Did he attribute Alice Kane's death to that, a strange death by all accounts. And Mickey Hendle's, the gardener's, too?

Or was he himself struggling against a belief in the curse?

I searched the faces of those at the table with me, wondering what lay behind the controlled masks they presented to me.

Dwayne had asked me to go on with the deception for a little while. I felt that I had to do so, for his sake.

Before it had been for Fabriana, to save her from her own folly, as it has become more and more clear.

But where was Fabriana now?

What was she doing?

Why hadn't she returned to make the exchange in the motel after the two weeks I had promised her were up?

Why had there been no word from her except that so unsatisfactory phone call?

I understood the call now. She must have been simply reassuring herself that I was still at Skeleton Key, and would stay there for as long as she wanted me to.

I thought again of the cheap brooch that Fabriana had stolen, of the heart hunger that had led her to it, of the fear that had kept her from admitting.

I trusted her, Dwayne had said.

Did that mean he had told her the truth about the Mayeroni treasure? Had she become heart hungry over the pictures in her mind of jewels and gold? Was that why her life had been endangered as long as she was on Skeleton Key? Was that why my own life was endangered now?

Had Fabriana really intended that I, as her stand-in, be sacrificed for some goal I didn't yet see clearly?

Sickened by the thought, I pushed my nearly untouched food away.

"Not hungry?" Karen asked without much concern.

Mark cut in, "It looks as if none of us are."

I rose. I just couldn't sit through any more

meaningless conversation. I excused myself, knowing the others were wondering, and went back to my room.

One thing, at least, I could do for Dwayne, was attend to the small amount of mail that he had managed to mark out replies to.

I settled down to work, glad to have something that would occupy my time, and my mind.

Unfortunately it was just for a little while. When I finished, I took the letters to Dwayne for his signature.

He was still sitting at his desk, very much as I had left him earlier, his face pale and his shoulders slumped.

He thanked me absently as he straightened, signed his name. "It seems so unimportant now."

"But you do have to get the book done, Dwayne."

"Yes. I suppose I do. Some way or another I do have to finish the accursed thing. After that . . . " He stopped himself.

"After that?" I asked.

He smiled faintly. "Why worry about a future that may never come?"

Later I was to remember those words.

I was to ask myself if he had known, guessed, what was to happen.

But then I said briskly, "We have to make

plans, to think, as if we know the future *will* come."

"Yes. You'd think that, wouldn't you? You're really so different inside. Different from Fabriana, I mean. I should have known it immediately. I should have felt it. Fabriana's a hedonist. She has to have her gratification immediately, and before anything else. That's why it's so hard to believe . . . "

I waited, hoping he would go on.

But he sighed, allowed that sentence to die. He bent his head, mumbled to the desk top, "But I don't believe it. Not really. You see, that's part of the trouble. I just can't believe it. And when I look at you . . . " Again he stopped. He looked up at me, his eyes suddenly sharp and concentrating. "Listen, tell me the truth. It's terribly important. So trust me, and tell me. Did Fabriana give you any idea, any hint, of whom she was afraid, of what she was afraid?"

"If I could, I would tell you," I answered. "I think you already know that, Dwayne. I hope you do. But she wasn't specific. She wasn't willing to be. When I came here I had no idea of which way to look. At first she said she was frightened and needed me. But then she said she wasn't. She just wanted a couple of weeks off, to . . . to . . . " I didn't finish. I didn't want to hurt Dwayne more. It didn't seem necessary to tell him that Fabriana had finally said she wanted to spend those two weeks with a man she was interested in, and wanted to keep her job to come back to. I didn't believe it anyway. She had stayed close to Key West. Karen had had a glimpse of her in Casey's bar more than likely, even though Hank had insisted Karen was wrong. But the phone call proved that Fabriana was still nearby. I picked up finally, with, "Well, anyway, I don't know what it was really about, Dwayne."

He nodded, then dismissed me. "But you'll be careful? I know what I'm asking when I ask you to go on with this charade. I'm quite sure you're safe. I've taken, and will take, further steps. But still, I want you to be quite careful. It's only for a little longer. I promise you that."

Later I remembered, too, how gentle his voice had been when he made that promise to me.

Later I wondered what steps he had taken, what he had hoped to do, planned to do, to resolve the mystery of Skeleton Key.

But I never knew.

By late afternoon the hazy sun was gone behind thick dark lowering clouds.

I lingered near the shell-lined path waiting

227

for Hank to return. The cove seemed to heave restlessly, casting up small showers of spray. The buoys tolled in their slow rhythm, and bobbed restlessly on either side of the narrow channel. The air was quite still then, but I felt a deepening pressure, as if a weighty mass bore more and more firmly upon the earth.

The launch came slowly into view, just when I was about to give up. It slid past the buoys and Hank raised his hand in an acknowledging wave.

He brought it into the marina, tied it up, and jumped out.

I had started down the path by then.

He came quickly to meet me.

"There's really going to be a storm," he said, jerking his head toward the cove. "It's a lot choppier than it looks."

"Did you get your errands done all right?"

He took my arm, turned me, led me back up the path to the house. "Mostly. I cut the trip short when I saw how the weather was going."

"It doesn't seem bad," I said. "Except for the sultriness."

"The false calm." He grinned. "You remember what it's like from last year."

Again I had the feeling that he was reminding me that I had been on the island for a year. I had been through a season of tropical storms.

"Oh, yes," I answered. "I certainly do remember."

I wished I knew what he had done in Key West, but I couldn't think of any way to ask him without being too obvious about it. I decided that I would have a look at the launch as soon as I could.

Hank left me and went in search of Karen, he said.

I waited for a few moments, then decided to go back down to the marina.

But when I went outside, I saw Hank coming back up the path again.

I knew there was no use searching the launch. He had gone back, done whatever it was that he wanted, taken whatever it was that he wanted.

I retreated to the patio where I would be within sight of Dwayne's windows, within shout of Mark's. It seemed strange to sit there in the heavy stillness, listening to a high hard humming sound that seemed to have no source.

I was alone until Karen came stamping through the small patio, and up to the gate, and leaned on it, staring at me.

"How did you do it, Fabriana?" she demanded.

I blinked at her. "What?"

"You know what I mean."

I shook my head.

She opened the gate, moved through it, and slammed it behind her. She came around the length of the pool, and stood over me.

"Look, I know I'm not seeing things. Not ten minutes ago you were out back near the workroom, wearing a black jersey and black jeans. And now you're right here, in a black jersey all right, but in a blue skirt instead. So please don't pretend you've been sitting here for hours. What are you doing all that skipping around for? That's what I want to know."

My heart began to beat very quickly.

I had been sitting in that chair for the past hour. I had been wearing a black jersey and a blue skirt all day.

Fabriana . . .

She must be on the island.

I remembered that morning. There had been a phone call. Rosa had said it was a wrong number. Suppose the wrong number was a signal to Hank. Suppose he had taken the launch to Key West and brought Fabriana back with him. Suppose that was why he had hurried me away from the launch, while she lay hidden until she could escape. Suppose he had gone back alone to make sure that she was gone?

But why would Fabriana have returned this way?

Was she intending now to make the change with me?

I had to see her, talk to her as quickly as I could.

But Karen was still standing over me, glaring angrily.

I put anger into my voice. I said, "I don't know that I have to explain my actions to you, Karen. I pulled on my black jeans because I was going to take the canoe out after all. Then when I saw how the cove looked, I decided against it, and changed back into my skirt, and sat down here. You didn't see me ten minutes ago. It was more like half an hour. If that doesn't satisfy you, then nothing will." I didn't wait for her response. I leaned back and closed my eyes, pretending to a calm I didn't feel.

"It sure is funny," she said doubtfully.

I shrugged. After a moment, I heard her walk away.

Dwayne didn't appear during the rest of the afternoon, nor later in the evening. But the others were always about. I waited anxiously for an opportunity to be alone. I wanted to check the workroom. I wanted to walk through the two patios, to circle the house, to see if I could possibly find Fabriana. It was quite hopeless.

I knew that Karen was watching me, her blue eyes sharp with malice.

Hank suggested bridge, and when I tried to escape it, Charlotte turned his suggestion into what was a politely veiled order. Karen made it a foursome, while Mark retired to the sofa and sat eyeing us over a magazine he only pretended to read.

We played for two hours. Then, with no attempt at courtesy, I threw in my hand, and escaped to my room, leaving the others either to amuse themselves with more cards or to go to sleep.

It was nearly midnight.

I was in bed, but reading, to pass the time.

By then I had heard Mark close his door. I had heard Karen and Hank talking, then go into their respective rooms. Charlotte had retired long before.

My own door was locked.

I had searched the room from corner to corner, searched the closet, peered under the bed, after I returned from the main house.

Everything was as I had left it. I had settled down to wait until no one was about. Then I was determined to go out into the darkness, determined to find Fabriana.

I had changed into dark pants, put on sneakers. I hoped I would be able to move freely and quickly and unobserved through the night.

I read a line or two without understanding, then looked at my wrist watch. Only moments had passed since my last glance at it.

There was a faint tap at my door. I dropped the book, sat up, swinging my feet to the floor.

The tap came again.

I crossed to the door, asked, "Who is it?" my voice a shaky breathless whisper.

Mark answered. "I saw your light. Can't you sleep?"

"I was just getting ready to turn it out."

"Want to take a quick walk?"

I did want to. It would have been pleasant to be able to stroll through the night, to feel safe enough to do so. But I did not dare challenge the dark alone with him, not with him, nor with anyone. And besides, I knew that the longer he spent with me, the longer I would have to wait before I could go out later alone.

"I guess not," I said finally. "I'll go to bed now."

He said good night, and I heard his footsteps fade down the path. Then I heard the click of his door closing.

I waited for a long time, listening with held breath.

There was nothing. Nothing but the steady snap of the palm fronds as they danced in the rising wind.

Then I heard a whisper that was not the

wind, and a splash that seemed to come from the pool.

The sound was like a wound burning through me.

I eased my door open. For a moment, I hesitated. Perhaps this was another instant of danger. Perhaps I was meant to be awakened, to be drawn out into the night. Perhaps someone was waiting for me.

But it might be Fabriana, hoping I would recognize her signal.

I couldn't refuse my anxiety. I stepped outside into heavy darkness. The hot thick pressure of the wind startled me. I took one step, then another. The shadows were close, heavy, blinding.

I moved toward the pool as if drawn on the invisible strands of intuition.

One step, then another.

I expected a blow from the dark, was braced to receive it. I moved slowly, carefully, wincing in awful anticipation, yet unable to turn back.

I heard a clear rustle of movement somewhere in the patio, and froze for a moment. Then the thick hard wind snapped the coconut fronds overhead.

I found myself at the edge of the pool, staring into inky darkness.

Something drifted there, something that

cast a darker shadow on the still-rippling surface.

I knelt, reached out with unwilling hands. My fingertips brushed a rounded hairy surface.

A scream rose in my throat. I fought it back, and cupped my hands, and the scream became a crazy impulse to laugh.

I drew the coconut from the pool, and set it on the terrazzo, and got to my feet just in time.

A tall slender form was moving in the small patio. I recognized its walk as it approached the low wooden gate, passed through it, and came toward me.

Chapter 14

I was immobilized by disappointment. It wasn't Fabriana.

It was Karen. Her tall slender form. Her gliding walk, but silent now.

Perhaps she had tossed the coconut into the pool, to draw me out of my room.

I found strength and courage. Silently I edged back, dodging carefully from shadow to shadow. Silently I gained the shelter of my room. I stepped inside, closed and locked the door behind me. I leaned there, breathing hard, but listening.

There was nothing but the wind, the snap of coconut fronds.

If Karen was still walking in the night, I could no longer hear her.

If Fabriana was hiding somewhere I didn't dare to go search her out. But she, I realized, would know that I was in my room. She would know where to find me.

I decided to wait for her. I lay on the bed, fully dressed still, and struggled with half-sleeping half-waking dreams of firelight and gold-hung savages fighting over a cheap tarnished medallion . . .

The room glowed with the pale orange of a dying flame, a cloudy dawn filtering through the drapes at the window.

A high keening wind exploded at the glass and shook the walls.

A high keening wind, and riding with it, a shrill and distant scream . . .

I jerked awake and on my feet in a single moment of consciousness, in a single movement.

I unlocked the door, then, once again I hesitated.

Was this a ploy to draw me out into the dangerous emptiness of morning?

Could this be, as the coconut dropped in the pool might have been, a trick to lead me to my death?

Fear froze me. But only for a moment. I had to know who had screamed on the wind, I had to know why. I unlocked the door.

At the same time I heard the sound of boots thumping on the path, and the banging of the low wooden gate as the wind slammed it against the wall.

Karen's voice, harsh with excitement, came to me clearly. "Dad," she said. "Wake up. You've got to come. It's Mayeroni. Something awful has happened to Fabriana!"

Fabriana!

I stepped outside.

Karen was struggling with Dwayne's door, still calling to him in a hoarse whisper.

Beyond her shoulder I saw the gate to the small patio where Mayeroni stood swinging in the wind.

Fabriana!

Karen had Dwayne's door open, was inside now.

I moved quietly into the wispy cover of the gray dawn. The thick hot wind took me as if I were a leaf, spun me along the patio, then fetched me up against the wall.

I made my way through the open gate, searching in the shadows of the lush greenery.

It was strangely different, altered in some way that I didn't at first recognize.

Then I realized that Mayeroni was gone!

The small statue no longer stood with arms outspread, and carved eyes fixed on the sky.

Behind me I heard Karen's voice carried on the wind, but couldn't understand the words. I heard Dwayne answer her.

I took one more step into the small patio, peering at the place where Mayeroni had been.

My scream tore the fabric of the high keening wind like a blade ripping velvet. It hung over the patio, reverberating against cedar and glass and stucco.

The stone Mayeroni was down, broken jagged edges lifted to the sky. Beneath him, limp and battered and very still, lay a small figure clad in black jersey and black pants.

Fabriana . . .

I knew that she was dead.

My sister, my twin . . .

Had she sent me to this accursed place to die?

Had she returned to save me?

Her sightless eyes, partly veiled by blood, didn't answer me.

I would never know the truth.

Light suddenly paled the gray dawn. I was aware again of the wind, and footsteps cracking on the terrazzo. I was aware again of Karen's shrill voice, drawing closer.

"I heard a sound and went out. Mayeroni was down, and Fabriana was crushed, crushed to death, I tell you, under his weight."

Dwayne was saying, "Oh, no, no . . . " and nothing more than that.

Firm arms came around me, drew me up, drew me away from the sight of Fabriana's lifeless body.

Mark said quietly, "I think I understand it now."

I buried my face in his chest, whispering, "She's dead, Mark. Fabriana's dead. I can't help her any more."

He didn't answer. He held me gently against him. Unaccountably I could feel strength flow from him into me. I felt his pulse become my pulse, and his courage my courage, and I thought of the love in his voice when he spoke of Alice Kane.

And it was then that Karen and Dwayne entered the small patio. She moved quickly, dancing ahead of him, shrill, impatient, wildly excited. He moved very slowly, laboriously, his face broken into lines I had never seen there before, the mahogany of his skin bleached green.

Karen turned pointing, and saw Mark and me standing together over the fallen figure of Mayeroni, over my twin's still body.

Her voice went silent. Her blue eyes widened. A white froth appeared at her snarling lips. "You're dead!" she screamed. "I killed you with my own hands and pushed him down on top of you. You're dead. Mayeroni killed you. Lie down again. You're dead!"

Behind her, Dwayne suddenly swayed. He threw back his head and clutched his throat, and then he fell. He fell like a big tree axed to the ground. He lay still, his chest heaving and big veins pulsing in his forehead.

Karen dropped down beside him, clutched his shoulders, shook him. "Dad," she cried.

"Dad, Dad? It's all right. She's really dead now. It's all right. We can be the same as always."

Hank and Charlotte were suddenly there, though I didn't remember seeing them appear.

They knelt for a moment beside Dwayne. Then Hank got to his feet and ran into the main house, muttering something about a doctor as he passed Mark and me.

I was finally able to move. I stepped from Mark's encircling arms, instantly feeling the impact of loneliness. I closed the small distance between Dwayne and me, and went down on my knees beside him.

Karen snarled, "Get away from him," and flung herself at me.

But Charlotte seized her, held her struggling body.

Dwayne's closed eyes fluttered open. His bluish lips moved. "Cecily," he whispered hoarsely, "Cecily, forgive me. I always knew. When Caroline died . . . the accident. I knew then. She's mad, has always been mad. Poor Fabriana, Alice . . . What could I do?"

His hoarse whisper ended on a choked breath. His mouth sagged open. His eyes stared at the lowering clouds above us. He was an old man suddenly, shrunken to half his size within his clothes. I knew then that he was dead.

Hank returned at that moment. He muttered a few words to Mark again. Later I learned that he hadn't been able to reach the mainland. The phone lines were down between the Key and the town. But then I was watching Karen.

Her wide blue eyes were fixed on Dwayne's still face. She had stopped struggling against Charlotte. She slipped away from her, leaned over her father. "No, no, it can't be. It just can't be," she whispered. She held up her hands, peered at them. "I tell you, it can't be. He isn't dead. I know he isn't. I didn't kill him." Her face, gaunt as a skeleton's, the blonde hair wind-plastered to her skull, tilted up. "You, Fabriana, yes, yes, I killed you. Why are you standing there? Why are you staring at me? I saw you sneaking through the patio, and I grabbed a rock and I hit you. You fell down without making a sound. I pushed Mayeroni over on you. Why are you standing there?" She shook her head from side to side, and her froth-limned lips twisted bitterly.

"No," Charlotte cried. "She's in shock. She doesn't know what she's saying. She didn't kill anybody. It was Mayeroni. It has to be. Dwayne didn't know . . . he wouldn't listen . . . but the old men said . . . " She stopped suddenly. She stared at me, then stared beyond me to where Fabriana lay. "I don't

242

understand," she murmured at last.

I was sorry for her. I knew that she had always preferred to believe in the efficacy of an ancient curse than to believe what she must have guessed long before.

I no longer feared the revenge of Mayeroni. It wasn't a long dead priest reaching through the ages to strike down his enemies that had threatened Fabriana, threatened me. It was warm flesh and blood and a mind gone into ruin.

Fabriana had never feared Mayeroni, I realized now. But she had feared that terrible jealousy which had finally struck her down. She had known of it, but had not known its source. Dwayne had said he had trusted her, confided in her. She must have known, or guessed, perhaps even been told, the truth about the treasure. She had feared that death would steal it from her. She had sent me to Skeleton Key to take her place, hoping, I wanted to believe, that I would unmask her enemy for her. And that then she would return to claim safely those golden ornaments and jewels she had always coveted.

Karen rose to her feet. She pressed her fists to her temples. "Why are you all staring at me?" She took a deep sobbing breath, and words like poison spewed from between her lips. "He was mine," she said. "He was. But

she was always with him. Don't you understand? Caroline, my mother, she left no room
in his life for me. They went on the digs together, and I had to stay in school. Me, alone,
in school. While they were together. It was
the two of them, always, always, against me. I
tried to make her see I belonged with them.
She laughed at me. She said, 'You're just a
little girl. You don't know what you want.'
We were driving to the house from shopping.
Buying things for her to get ready to go with
him again. We were arguing because she
wouldn't listen. She just kept laughing. I hit
her with a flashlight, and yanked the wheel.
She was driving too fast, of course, to get back
to him. She was thrown out of the car. I made
sure. But I was okay . . . "

Charlotte whispered, "No, Karen. Karen,
stop it. It's all fantasy. It's what you imagined. You didn't, you didn't, I tell you . . . "

But Karen went on, "I went with him myself. It was good then. The way it was supposed to be. The two of us together. But then
I realized it wasn't. Alice Kane. Green-eyed,
man-hungry. She couldn't let him alone."

Mark stirred beside me. He made a small
pained sound.

I took his hand, offering him mute sympathy for what he must feel.

He gave me an unfathomable glance,

244

drew me closer to him.

"Alice. Oh, yes, I knew what was going on. And when we came back here I knew what to do. I waited, until the time was right, and I smashed her head with a coconut. I stood in the shadows of the trees, and when she passed, I threw it as hard as I could. She never knew what hit her. Everybody thought it was an accident. Except Mickey. I didn't know he was out there, too. He didn't see anything, but he mentioned how there had been no wind. He couldn't understand it. He was easy to handle. He had a yen for me. I took him down to the shore, to go fishing. I pushed him in and stood on him until it was over. It didn't matter. Neither of them did. Just Dwayne. And then, then he betrayed me again. He turned to Fabriana. I tried to scare her away. I got into her room and dumped out her clothes. I put ground glass in her orange juice. Charlotte said it was Mayeroni. But of course it was me. Fabriana just laughed about it. Like Caroline. She just laughed. She had her own plans. She thought I didn't know them. But she did. She canoed around the island to meet Hank. You didn't know I knew about that, did you, Hank?"

He gave her a dazed look, shook his head from side to side.

Karen's sobbing laugh became words

245

again. "Oh, yes, I followed them. I saw them. They were up to something. But I didn't care what. I just wanted to get rid of her. So I fixed the wardrobe. She should have been crushed to death, but she managed to escape me. I put a hole in the canoe and patched it. She should have drowned. But Mark saved her. I found a black widow by accident and left it in her room. But Mark found it. I knew today, this morning, when he wanted to talk to her. I knew Dwayne had decided to marry her. So I decided that I'd kill her tonight. I stayed up after I missed my chance at the workroom. I just stayed up, waiting. But I couldn't get at her. I dropped a coconut in the pool. But she didn't come out. Then, later, I realized that she had somehow gotten past me. She was in the small patio. I found her there." The wide blue eyes sought me out. "Tell them, Fabriana. Tell them that you're dead."

"My sister," I answered quietly. "It is my sister Fabriana that's lying here, Karen. Your father realized that this morning. Realized, I mean, that I am Cecily Harden. That I was only pretending to be Fabriana."

"No," Karen whispered. "No. I don't believe it." Her wide eyes sought reassurance from Charlotte, then Hank, then Mark.

None of them answered her.

Finally Hank said, "It's all over."

"You knew all along," I told him. "You and Fabriana must have planned it together."

"I didn't do anything," he retorted. "It was all Fabriana's idea. She realized that the Mayeroni myth must have a kernel of truth in it somewhere. She went to work on Dwayne. I guess he told her enough to whet her appetite. Then these crazy things started happening. She got scared, but not scared enough to give up. She told me about getting you down here, and warned me to play along. I helped her out that way. I admit that. Why not? She asked, so I helped her out. When she signaled me with that wrong number yesterday I went in to town. She said she'd changed her mind. She was coming back to the island to talk to you, Cecily. So I brought her. You almost found her then, but she was determined that nobody else know. She was going to step back into her own shoes maybe. I don't know that for sure. Anyhow, she hid out in the work-room. And that's the last I saw of her." He stopped, swallowed, forced his mouth into a painful grin. "It's all finished now. With her dead, and Dwayne dead, too, nobody will ever find the Mayeroni treasure now."

"He wins," Charlotte moaned. "I told you. I told you. It's just as the old men said."

In the silence that followed her words the high keening wind became more shrill, the coconut fronds snapped, the palmettos rustled, as the hard hot pressure swept through the small patio.

We all stirred in response.

But Karen swayed close to me, peered into my face, then she stumbled over to where Fabriana lay and peered down at her.

"Two of them," she muttered. "Yes. Two." She rose stiffly, moved away like a sleepwalker.

Mark reached for her, and she screamed. She slipped from his grasp and spun off, racing away, fleeing, with her screams trailing her faintly on the wind.

Mark, I, the others, ran after her, but madness made her quick. It drove her to the marina. The cove was rimmed with white, and was swollen. From far away, it seemed, there came the slow deep tolling of the buoys at the channel. The intermittent lights blinked through the gray gloom.

She cast off, and the tides took the launch beyond reach.

Standing helplessly on the shore, we heard the motor catch, roar briefly, and die. The launch was swept on toward the channel, and then beyond it. Then it rocked and shook and climbed a coral shelf. It stood straight up, a grim silhouette against the sky, before it exploded into brief brilliance. Within moments it settled and slipped, steaming, into the white-rimmed seas. Karen was gone forever.

I shuddered and turned away.

A few hours later, the wind had died, the sun was out. Mark was able to establish contact with the town by phone.

Soon after, a doctor came to examine Dwayne's body. He ascribed Dwayne's death to an apparent heart attack. He knelt beside Fabriana's body for a long time, then rose to tell us that a fractured skull had killed her and that he must report it to the police who were already on the way to investigate the sinking of the launch and the loss of Karen with it.

I realized then that I would have to tell them the truth. I couldn't hold back or lie. We gathered in the sunlit dining room. I was relieved when Mark suggested to the officers that he begin. At their nods, he glanced at me. He said, "I came here to Skeleton Key two months ago. Ostensibly to ghost write Dwayne Fuller's book, after Alice Kane's death. My real reason was to investigate her death." He gave me another glance, a longer one this time. "Alice Kane was my sister."

Warmth, mixed with pity, swept me. The love in his voice when he spoke her name had been the love of a brother for a sister.

He went on, "I knew she cared deeply for

Dwayne, but her letters were vaguely troubled. I couldn't understand why. When she died I was determined to find out."

Then it was my turn. I told them everything I knew just as I've written it down here.

I was packing. I filled the weekend case only with those few things that I would need for my trip home. Everything else of Fabriana's I was leaving for Charlotte to dispose of as she wished.

I had taken off the false eyelashes, washed away the shadow, scrubbed the bright lipstick off my lips the night before. In the terror that had come with dawn, I had never replaced them. I knew I never would. I would never try to wear Fabriana's face again.

Poor Fabriana. She had been weak, weak all her life. Now she was dead. I would never know whether she had come back to sacrifice me on the altar of her greed or whether she had come back to save me before it was too late.

I was free.

I was alone.

A curious emptiness surrounded me.

Then Mark spoke softly from the doorway. "Cecily?"

I turned to look at him, sudden joy suffusing me. It was good, at least, to be able to look ing me. It was good, at least, to be able to look at him one last time. Good to know that this time I would be able to say goodbye properly.

He said, "I feel as if I have to get to know you all over again."

"You suspected the truth, didn't you?"

"A part of me must have. I thought that there'd been such a sudden change in Fabriana. I couldn't understand it. That's why I did so much following you about. Why I kept turning up whenever anything happened." He paused. Then, "These past three weeks, you see, I found myself so . . . so attracted . . . Before that, with Fabriana . . ." He shrugged. "Naturally I wondered who had changed. And why."

I waited.

"I like a place where there are seasons," he went on gently. "I like red maples in the fall, and golden oaks. I like a cold morning sun, and snow at Christmas, and . . ."

"It'll be that way at home," I said tentatively.

He gave me a wide white grin. "I know," he said. "Maybe that's why I'm going with you."

A few minutes later, we left Skeleton Key together.

We turned our backs forever on the Mayeroni myth.

The employees of THORNDIKE PRESS hope you have enjoyed this Large Print book. All our Large Print titles are designed for easy reading, and all our books are made to last. Other Thorndike Large Print books are available at your library, through selected bookstores, or directly from us. For more information about current and upcoming titles, please call or mail your name and address to:

THORNDIKE PRESS
PO Box 159
Thorndike, Maine 04986
800/223-6121
207/948-2962

LT W783may   c.1

Winston, Daoma, 1922-

The Mayeroni myth

TC15,582 $16.25

lg print
Win

Winston, Daoma
The Mayeroni myth.